The Earl Rin

She was lovelier, the Earl th.
had seen for a long time.

He sat down on one side of the bed and asked:

"Are you asleep, or only pretending?"

Donela opened her eyes.

She looked at the Earl and gave a distinct start
before she said:

"What . . . has . . . happened . . . what is . . .
wrong?"

"There is nothing wrong," the Earl replied, "except that one of my guests went to bed without saying
goodnight."

It took Donela a second to understand what he was
saying.

Then she replied:

"I . . . I thought it was . . . best. But . . . why are
you . . . here?"

"I should have thought that was obvious," the Earl
replied. . . .

A Camfield Novel of Love
by Barbara Cartland

---

*"Barbara Cartland's novels are all distinguished by their
intelligence, good sense, and good nature . . ."*
— **ROMANTIC TIMES**

*"Who could give better advice on how to keep your romance
going strong than the world's most famous romance novelist, Barbara Cartland?"*
— **THE STAR**

Camfield Place,
Hatfield
Hertfordshire,
England

Dearest Reader,

Camfield Novels of Love mark a very exciting era of my books with Jove. They have already published nearly two hundred of my titles since they became my first publisher in America, and now all my original paperback romances in the future will be published exclusively by them.

As you already know, Camfield Place in Hertfordshire is my home, which originally existed in 1275, but was rebuilt in 1867 by the grandfather of Beatrix Potter.

It was here in this lovely house, with the best view in the county, that she wrote *The Tale of Peter Rabbit*. Mr. McGregor's garden is exactly as she described it. The door in the wall that the fat little rabbit could not squeeze underneath and the goldfish pool where the white cat sat twitching its tail are still there.

I had Camfield Place blessed when I came here in 1950 and was so happy with my husband until he died, and now with my children and grandchildren, that I know the atmosphere is filled with love and we have all been very lucky.

It is easy here to write of love and I know you will enjoy the Camfield Novels of Love. Their plots are definitely exciting and the covers very romantic. They come to you, like all my books, with love.

Bless you,

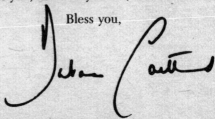

CAMFIELD NOVELS OF LOVE
by *Barbara Cartland*

THE POOR GOVERNESS
WINGED VICTORY
LUCKY IN LOVE
LOVE AND THE MARQUIS
A MIRACLE IN MUSIC
LIGHT OF THE GODS
BRIDE TO A BRIGAND
LOVE COMES WEST
A WITCH'S SPELL
SECRETS
THE STORMS OF LOVE
MOONLIGHT ON THE SPHINX
WHITE LILAC
REVENGE OF THE HEART
THE ISLAND OF LOVE
THERESA AND A TIGER
LOVE IS HEAVEN
MIRACLE FOR A MADONNA
A VERY UNUSUAL WIFE
THE PERIL AND THE PRINCE
ALONE AND AFRAID
TEMPTATION OF A TEACHER
ROYAL PUNISHMENT
THE DEVILISH DECEPTION
PARADISE FOUND
LOVE IS A GAMBLE
A VICTORY FOR LOVE
LOOK WITH LOVE
NEVER FORGET LOVE
HELGA IN HIDING

SAFE AT LAST
HAUNTED
CROWNED WITH LOVE
ESCAPE
THE DEVIL DEFEATED
THE SECRET OF THE
  MOSQUE
A DREAM IN SPAIN
THE LOVE TRAP
LISTEN TO LOVE
THE GOLDEN CAGE
LOVE CASTS OUT FEAR
A WORLD OF LOVE
DANCING ON A RAINBOW
LOVE JOINS THE CLANS
AN ANGEL RUNS AWAY
FORCED TO MARRY
BEWILDERED IN BERLIN
WANTED—A WEDDING RING
THE EARL ESCAPES
STARLIGHT OVER TUNIS
THE LOVE PUZZLE
LOVE AND KISSES
SAPPHIRES IN SIAM
A CARETAKER OF LOVE
SECRETS OF THE HEART
RIDING IN THE SKY
LOVERS IN LISBON
LOVE IS INVINCIBLE
THE GODDESS OF LOVE

AN ADVENTURE OF LOVE
THE HERB FOR HAPPINESS
ONLY A DREAM
SAVED BY LOVE
LITTLE TONGUES OF FIRE
A CHIEFTAIN FINDS LOVE
THE LOVELY LIAR
THE PERFUME OF THE GODS
A KNIGHT IN PARIS
REVENGE IS SWEET
THE PASSIONATE PRINCESS
SOLITA AND THE SPIES
THE PERFECT PEARL
LOVE IS A MAZE
A CIRCUS FOR LOVE
THE TEMPLE OF LOVE
THE BARGAIN BRIDE
THE HAUNTED HEART
REAL LOVE OR FAKE
KISS FROM A STRANGER
A VERY SPECIAL LOVE
THE NECKLACE OF LOVE
A REVOLUTION OF LOVE
THE MARQUIS WINS
LOVE IS THE KEY
LOVE AT FIRST SIGHT
THE TAMING OF A TIGRESS
PARADISE IN PENANG
THE EARL RINGS A BELLE

Other Books by *Barbara Cartland*

THE ADVENTURER
AGAIN THIS RAPTURE
BARBARA CARTLAND'S
  BOOK OF BEAUTY AND
  HEALTH
BLUE HEATHER
BROKEN BARRIERS
THE CAPTIVE HEART
THE COIN OF LOVE
THE COMPLACENT WIFE
COUNT THE STARS
DESIRE OF THE HEART
DESPERATE DEFIANCE
THE DREAM WITHIN
ELIZABETHAN LOVER
THE ENCHANTED WALTZ
THE ENCHANTING EVIL
ESCAPE FROM PASSION
FOR ALL ETERNITY
A GOLDEN GONDOLA
A HAZARD OF HEARTS
A HEART IS BROKEN
THE HIDDEN HEART

THE IRRESISTIBLE BUCK
THE KISS OF PARIS
THE KISS OF THE DEVIL
A KISS OF SILK
THE KNAVE OF HEARTS
THE LEAPING FLAME
A LIGHT TO THE HEART
LIGHTS OF LOVE
THE LITTLE PRETENDER
LOST ENCHANTMENT
LOVE AT FORTY
LOVE FORBIDDEN
LOVE IN HIDING
LOVE TO THE RESCUE
LOVE UNDER FIRE
THE MAGIC OF HONEY
METTERNICH THE
  PASSIONATE DIPLOMAT
MONEY, MAGIC AND
  MARRIAGE
NO HEART IS FREE
THE ODIOUS DUKE

OPEN WINGS
A RAINBOW TO HEAVEN
THE RELUCTANT BRIDE
THE SCANDALOUS LIFE OF
  KING CAROL
THE SMUGGLED HEART
A SONG OF LOVE
STARS IN MY HEART
STOLEN HALO
SWEET PUNISHMENT
THEFT OF A HEART
THE THIEF OF LOVE
THIS TIME IT'S LOVE
TOUCH A STAR
TOWARDS THE STARS
THE UNKNOWN HEART
WE DANCED ALL
  NIGHT
THE WINGS OF ECSTASY
THE WINGS OF LOVE
WINGS ON MY HEART
WOMAN, THE ENIGMA

A NEW CAMFIELD NOVEL OF LOVE BY

BARBARA CARTLAND

The Earl Rings a Belle

JOVE BOOKS, NEW YORK

THE EARL RINGS A BELLE

A Jove Book / published by arrangement with
the author

PRINTING HISTORY
Jove edition / December 1990

For information address: The Berkley Publishing Group,
200 Madison Avenue, New York, New York 10016.

ISBN: 0-515-10476-0

Jove Books are published by The Berkley Publishing Group,
200 Madison Avenue, New York, New York 10016.
The name "JOVE" and the "J" logo
are trademarks belonging to Jove Publications, Inc.

PRINTED IN THE UNITED STATES OF AMERICA

10 9 8 7 6 5 4 3 2 1

Author's Note

IN mediaeval days, Tumblers and Musicians amused the nobles in the strongholds.

Minstrels going from place to place carried news of victories or defeats between the Clans.

In London there were the famous Pleasure Gardens. At one time there were 200 round Greater London alone, and these like Vauxhall Gardens became the favourite pick-up for the Mashers, Swells, and Blades of the time.

By 1820 there were innumerable Taverns like the Coal Hole, Cider, and Cider Cellars where there were singers, sketches, conjuring acts, and a strip-tease entitled "Plastic Poses."

By 1860 the most important of these was Evans's "Song and Supper Room" in Covent Garden.

As a rule, the bills were changed every week, and from the Supper Rooms there emerged the Music Halls, where there were the seats and not the tables for eating and drinking.

Tights were first introduced in America in 1850, and caused an outcry of horror. People protested about them and they were condemned as immodest and immoral beyond words.

The public outcry was loud and prolonged. In fact, tights became synonymous with sin.

When eventually they came to London, they were used in the "Pose Plastique," which had come from the Continent, but the women who portrayed them were, until they adopted tights, not allowed to move.

They were, needless to say, not seen or even talked of by any woman who considered herself a Lady.

The Earl Rings a Belle

chapter one

1869

DONELA came into the house feeling happy.

She had enjoyed a wonderful ride over the Park.

Nothing, she thought, could be more lovely than the daffodils coming out under the trees, the primroses and violets nestling amongst the moss.

As she walked in through the front-door, the Butler came forward to say:

"Sir Marcus wishes to speak to you, Miss Donela."

Instinctively, Donela stiffened.

She wondered frantically what she could have done to incur her step-father's displeasure.

It must be something, or he would not have told the servants he wanted her.

She knew he would be waiting in his Study.

In her mind she always associated that particular

room with something wrong.

When Sir Marcus had to reprove a servant or herself, it always happened in the Study.

At the same time, she was fond of her step-father because he made her mother happy.

When Captain Angus Colwyn went down with his ship in an unusually fierce storm in the Bay of Biscay, his wife was heart-broken.

She was so upset that she almost followed him into the next world.

Apart from the fact that she had adored her husband and was distraught at losing him, she was also left with very little money.

A Naval Captain's pay was meagre, and there was only a tiny pension for his widow and children.

"I cannot think what we are to do, Donela," her mother said to her tearfully.

"We will manage somehow," Donela replied. "I know Papa would hate you to cry and make yourself ill."

Mrs. Colwyn made a tremendous effort to pull herself together for her daughter's sake.

She loved her and she knew she was going to be a very attractive young woman.

She often thought that Donela missed so much, living in rented accommodation in sea-ports.

There were few large houses in those areas, and the people who lived in them were not particularly impressed by a Sea-Captain and his wife.

Mrs. Colwyn's family were in Northumberland.

She had been the daughter of a popular and respected Country Squire.

One of a large family, she had been to innumerable Balls as a *débutante*.

While she had never come to London to make her curtsy to the Queen, she had met a great number of people socially.

Because she was very lovely, her father had thought she would marry well, preferably one of his rich and distinguished neighbours.

Unfortunately for him, on a visit to a Hall where she was attending a Ball, Mary Acton, as she was then, met Captain Angus Colwyn.

The moment he saw her he was bowled over and fell "head-over-heels" in love for the first time in his life.

Despite every protest from Mary's father, they were married before he went back to sea.

They went South so that she could wait at any port to which his ship was likely to return.

Mrs. Colwyn and Donela were living in Portsmouth when they learnt that Captain Colwyn had lost his life.

They had rented a small furnished house until they would be told to move to another part of the coast.

After her husband's death, Mrs. Colwyn had felt she could not bear to be anywhere near the sea.

How could she watch ships which did not carry her husband coming into harbour?

She had, therefore, for no particular reason except that somebody had told her it was cheap, moved to Worcestershire.

There they rented a small but very attractive black-and-white Elizabethan cottage.

It was on the outskirts of a pretty village, where they made friends amongst the villagers.

It was quite by chance that Mrs. Colwyn became friends with the Master of Foxhounds, the very distinguished Earl of Coventry.

Because she was a very pretty woman, the Earl lent her his horses to ride and she hunted with the Crome Pack.

The Earl and his wife, if short of a woman at dinner, would frequently invite Mrs. Colwyn to join them.

She always enjoyed these special occasions because they were so different from her somewhat humdrum existence.

It was at a party given after the Flower Show that she met Sir Marcus Grayson.

Just like Angus Colwyn, the moment he saw her he fell in love.

A man of fifty-five, he had been quite certain he would never marry again.

He had actually been a widower for over ten years.

He had found Mary Colwyn irresistible.

Almost before she had time to think of him as her suitor, he had asked her to marry him.

She was still grieving for her husband.

She felt she could never give her heart to anybody else, so her first impulse was to refuse him.

Then, as Sir Marcus persisted in pursuing her, she thought of her daughter.

Although she was fortunate enough to be friendly with the Coventrys, they had no children of Donela's age.

They never suggested that Mary Colwyn should bring her daughter to any of the festivities they arranged.

If she talked of Donela to the Countess, it was obvious she was not really interested.

Sir Marcus was a rich man and also very distinguished.

The 5th Baronet, he described to Mary the magnificent house he had in the North of Hertfordshire.

He was extremely proud of his large estate.

He also spent some of his time in London, where he was a guest of all the great hostesses.

At least two or three times a year he was invited by the Queen to Windsor Castle.

Mary Colwyn looked at Donela and knew that, apart from anything else, her education was not as good as it should be.

How could she afford Tutors such as she had enjoyed when she was young?

They had made her the equal of her brothers, who had been at Eton and Oxford.

Ultimately, because she loved her daughter, she succumbed to Sir Marcus's pleadings.

Delighted at having got his own way, as he always expected, they were married immediately.

It was a quiet wedding.

Because he did not want his friends to gossip and criticise, no one was invited to the Ceremony, not even Donela.

"I want you all to myself," Sir Marcus said to his bride. "And if I am the happiest man alive, which I believe myself to be, I will not share my happiness with anybody else.''

They went away on their honeymoon.

Donela was sent to the smartest and most exclusive Seminary for Young Ladies in London.

She was there for a year.

Then, because she suspected her step-father did not want her at home for the holidays, she went to what was called a "Finishing School" in Florence.

Because she had always wanted to travel, she was excited at the idea.

At the same time, she hated leaving her mother.

"I love you, Mama!" she said with tears in her eyes. "And I will miss being with you all the time, as we used to be when Papa was alive."

"I know, darling," Mary Grayson said, "but you know your step-father is jealous if I concern myself with anyone except him."

"But you are mine too," Donela objected, "and I was there first!"

Mary Grayson laughed gently.

Then her eyes were tender.

"I know exactly what you are saying, my precious," she answered, "but I have to do what your step-father wants, and as it has cost him a great deal of money to have you properly educated, you must show your gratitude."

"I am grateful," Donela said, "but in London I could come home for the holidays. Now Step-Papa says I am to stay in Florence for a year and six months without seeing you."

Her voice broke, and Lady Grayson put her arms

around her daughter and held her very close.

"Once you are grown up," she said, "things will be different. You will have friends of your own—the right sort of friends I have always wanted for you—and your step-father has promised to give a Ball for you both in London and in the country."

"But . . . it will not be the same as being with you, Mama," Donela sobbed.

Lady Grayson did not put what she was thinking into words.

She was sure, however, that by the time Donela came back to England, Sir Marcus would not be quite so possessive about her as he was now.

The year and a half in Florence passed slowly.

At the same time, Donela was sensible enough to realise she had an opportunity which would never come again.

Sir Marcus was very generous over extra tuition.

She was therefore able to learn a number of languages which were added to her curriculum besides dancing and riding.

She enjoyed, too, being with girls of every nationality.

She learnt about different countries and their customs from them as well as from books.

When finally, at Easter, she had come back to England, she was just eighteen.

Although she was not aware of it, she was far better educated than most English girls.

She had inherited her father's intelligence as well as his sense of adventure.

She had grown up in the time she had been abroad.

She had also become even lovelier than her mother remembered.

Now her large green eyes flecked with gold dominated her small, pointed face.

Her hair had fiery lights amongst the fair curls.

It was much admired by the Florentines and was different from that of most Englishwomen.

"You have become very beautiful, my darling!" Lady Grayson exclaimed with delight. "Oh, how I wish your father could see you now!"

"He would think I was very like you, Mama," Donela answered.

"Your hair is more spectacular than mine, and your eyes are greener," Lady Grayson said, "but after your father had seen me, he said he could never look at another woman."

She spoke with a little sob in her voice.

It was impossible even now after so long to talk of her first husband without wanting to cry.

Sometimes at night she would lie thinking of him.

She wished the years could go by quickly so that she could join him again.

But she told herself she was being ungrateful.

Sir Marcus doted on his wife and was very proud of her.

She had only to express a wish for it to be granted.

Her jewel-case was filled with the gifts he showered upon her.

If he had to go to London and she did not accompany him, he never returned without bringing her a new diamond brooch, a ring, or a necklace.

"You spoil me!" she would protest. "How can I ever thank you?"

"All I want is your love," Sir Marcus would say fiercely. "And I want all of it. I am jealous of every thought, and every breath you draw!"

She knew he suspected that she still mourned her first husband.

She was very careful never to mention him.

Nor did she talk about Angus Colwyn to Donela if Sir Marcus was there.

She was acutely aware, and so was Donela, that Sir Marcus was extremely jealous.

He even resented every moment that his wife spent with her daughter.

He continued to be generous to Donela.

Yet Mary Grayson knew that he was calculating in his mind how soon she could be married and he could be free of her.

Walking towards the Study, Donela was trying to think of something she had done which had annoyed her step-father.

Last night they had been alone at dinner.

Afterwards, so that Sir Marcus could talk to her mother without her being brought into the conversation, she had sat down at the piano.

She played very well.

At school the girls had competed several times a year in singing the modern songs that were popular in their various countries.

The French girls always won the contest because those they brought from Paris were gay and light-hearted.

The songs the German girls sang were far too serious.

Only the Italians came close to beating the French.

Donela lagged humiliatingly far behind the others.

Finally she wrote to her mother asking her to send her the popular songs of the moment.

Lady Grayson had taken a great deal of trouble.

She discovered those which were being sung in London in what were known as the "Music Halls."

They were a new development from the old Supper Rooms, where the people ate and drank.

When they did so, they were entertained by performers of all types and varieties.

There were acrobats, comedians and musicians, some professional, some amateur.

When the singers became popular, their songs were whistled and sung in the streets.

Whenever they appeared at the Music Hall, the audience applauded, cheered, and sang with them.

"Champagne Charlie" was one of the songs that had every errand-boy whistling it.

"Gilbert the Filbert" was another.

It was songs such as these that Lady Grayson sent to Florence.

The songs with their lilting tunes had captivated London.

They also enchanted the very aristocratic pupils in the Finishing School.

For the first time, the English won the contest.

'Perhaps Step-Papa thought what I was playing last night was too frivolous,' Donela thought as she reached the Study door. 'Tonight I will keep to the Classics.'

She went into the Study to find Sir Marcus was not sitting at his desk as she expected.

He was standing at the window, looking out into the garden.

He was a tall man, handsome in a very different way from her father.

Yet he was undoubtedly very distinguished-looking.

"I was told you wanted to see me, Step-Papa," Donela said in a rather small voice.

Sir Marcus turned round, and to her relief he was smiling.

"Did you enjoy your ride, Donela?" he enquired.

"It was wonderful!" Donela answered. "Your horses are superb and it is a joy to ride them!"

Sir Marcus reached the fireplace and stood with his back to it.

Although it was April and the sun was shining, it was still rather cold.

It could be chilly in the big house with its huge rooms and high ceilings.

The fires therefore were still lit just first thing in the morning.

"Sit down, Donela," Sir Marcus said, "I want to talk to you."

"About what, Step-Papa?" she asked. "I hope I have done nothing wrong."

"No, no, and you are a very lucky young woman!" Sir Marcus replied.

Donela looked at him enquiringly.

"Because I can ride your magnificent horses?"

"Something more important than that," he replied.

She waited for his explanation, wondering what it could be.

There was a short pause, as if he were choosing his words, before Sir Marcus said:

"Lord Waltingham called on me this morning, on his way to London, and we had a long talk together."

Donela wondered how this could possibly concern her.

Lord Waltingham was a close friend of her step-father's, and a very distinguished man.

He had an important position at Court and represented the Queen as the Lord Lieutenant of Hertfordshire.

He was very rich and came from a distinguished family.

She knew that this impressed Sir Marcus.

He was exceedingly proud of his own ancestry, but Lord Waltingham's ancestor had been made a Peer by Queen Elizabeth the First.

All down the centuries members of his family had served the nation faithfully, and been rewarded for their labours.

"You may be surprised to learn," Sir Marcus was saying, "that Lord Waltingham wanted to talk about you."

"About . . . me?" Donela exclaimed in astonishment.

Lord Waltingham had come to luncheon the previous day, and she tried to remember what he had said to her that could possibly concern her step-father.

Then she remembered he had said that his Labrador bitch, which was always with him in the country, had just produced a litter.

She smiled as she exclaimed:

"I know why he came to see you! He is going to offer me one of his puppies, but I feel, Step-Papa, it is something you would not want in the house."

"No," Sir Marcus said, "that is not what he came about. And I certainly do not want any dogs other than my own here!"

"Then . . . what did he want?" Donela asked curiously.

"This may come as a surprise to you, as it did to me," Sir Marcus answered, "but as I said, you are a very fortunate young woman because Lord Waltingham wishes you to become his wife!"

For a moment Donela thought she could not have heard aright.

She stared at Sir Marcus in sheer astonishment before she said the first words that came into her head.

"B-but . . . he is old . . . much too old . . . !"

Sir Marcus stiffened.

"His Lordship is the same age as myself, and I do not consider I am old."

"No . . . of course not . . . Step-Papa," Donela said quickly, "but you are married to my mother . . . and Lord Waltingham is old enough to be my . . . father!"

"I do not think that age really counts," Sir Marcus said. "Lord Waltingham is one of the most distinguished men in the County, extremely wealthy, admired, and respected by everybody with whom he comes in contact."

He paused for a moment before he said:

"You should go down on your knees, Donela, and thank God that you have the good fortune to marry such a man."

"But . . . I cannot . . . marry him!" Donela objected. "I hardly . . . know him . . . and . . . I do not . . . love him."

She was just about to say "and I could not love anybody so old."

Then she remembered that her step-father was sensitive about his age.

She therefore changed the words at the last minute.

"Am I to believe," Sir Marcus asked sharply, "that you are really refusing this offer?"

"As I have . . . already said," Donela answered, "I do not . . . love Lord Waltingham . . . and I could not marry any man . . . unless I . . . loved him!"

"Love? Love?" Sir Marcus said. "What do young women know about love? Love with a man like His Lordship will come after marriage—of course it will!"

"And . . . if it does not . . . what could . . . I do . . . about it?" Donela enquired.

There was silence.

She saw by the expression on her step-father's face that he was growing angry.

"I do not intend to argue with you about this, Donela. You see, I have already told Lord Waltingham that your mother and I will welcome him as your husband."

He looked at her to see if she was listening before he went on:

"He is coming here tomorrow afternoon to propose to you formally, and you will accept him!"

"And if . . . if I . . . refuse to . . . do so?" Donela asked hesitatingly.

"There can be no question of you doing anything as foolish as that," Sir Marcus replied.

"As I . . . have already . . . said—" Donela began.

"Now, listen, you stupid child," he interrupted, "as you should be aware, having lived abroad, marriage amongst the aristocrats is always arranged, and the same applies in England. As your Guardians, your mother and I can compel you to marry anyone we choose, and you have to obey!"

Donela jumped to her feet.

"How could you force me to do anything that would make me unhappy?" she asked. "Mama married Papa because she loved him. I do not believe that she would force me into marrying a man for whom I hold . . . no affection and I am quite certain I would dislike as . . . my husband."

"You are talking in an hysterical and idiotic manner!" Sir Marcus roared. "And let me make this clear—if you do not do as I say, you can leave my house and fend for yourself!"

His voice sharpened as he went on:

"Where do you think the money has come from for the clothes you wear, the food you eat, and the expensive education you have had?"

"Are . . . are you . . . saying that . . . you will not . . . keep me?" Donela asked.

"You have a choice," Sir Marcus answered. "Either you marry one of the richest men in England, or you support yourself as a Governess or Companion to some crotchety old lady!''

Donela knew there was no other situation open to women.

With a little sob she walked towards the window.

She stood with her back to the room, as her step-father had been doing.

Outside, the sun was shining on the garden.

The spring flowers made a brilliant patch of colour against the green of the lawns.

She knew that everything that belonged to her step-father was as perfect as his money could make it.

She thought how difficult it had been to make ends meet in their little black-and-white cottage after her father had been lost at sea.

Yet now she saw Lord Waltingham in a different way.

He was a big man with broad shoulders.

He had a high forehead from which the hair was beginning to recede.

It was grey over his temples and there were deep lines under his eyes and running down from his nose to his mouth.

He had been handsome when he was young.

He was still what people would call a "fine figure of a man."

At the same time, he was old, old enough for her never for one moment to have thought of him as a man who might want to touch or kiss her.

She felt herself shiver.

She knew she wanted to cry out in horror at the idea of being his wife.

How could she go through the rest of her life tied to him?

She knew now he was repugnant to her although she could not explain why.

"I . . . cannot do it . . . I cannot!" she said in her heart.

From behind her came her step-father's voice.

"Now, listen, Donela," he said. "I have no wish to upset you, and I know this has been a shock. But you are an intelligent girl and I know when you think it over you will realise how fortunate you are."

He paused a moment before continuing:

"You are honoured that Lord Waltingham has chosen you to be his wife out of all the women he knows."

Donela did not answer, and he went on:

"I expect you are aware that he was married once, but his wife became an invalid, and after lingering for some years, died of a wasting disease for which the Doctors could find no cure."

Still Donela did not speak or turn round, and Sir Marcus continued:

"It was then that Waltingham plunged himself heart and soul into working for his country. He has been brilliantly successful with every Diplomatic mission he undertook on behalf of Her Majesty and the Foreign Office. And he has worked untiringly for Hertfordshire."

Sir Marcus finished speaking, and after a moment Donela turned round.

"I think . . . Step-Papa," she said, "I should . . . discuss this . . . with Mama."

Sir Marcus's expression lightened.

"Of course, my dear—a very sensible attitude—and exactly what you should do. Besides, your mother is as delighted as I am that you should hold such an important position both at Court and here in the country."

"I will go to . . . her now," Donela said in a low voice.

She went from the room without looking at her step-father.

She shut the door behind her.

He told himself that everything had gone satisfactorily and exactly as he wanted it.

Of course the child, and it was difficult to think of her as grown up, would realise that she would never have a better offer.

Also, the sooner she was married, the sooner she would be off his hands.

At the same time, no one could complain that he had not procured the very best for his step-daughter.

'When Waltingham comes here tomorrow,' he thought as he sat down at his desk, 'we will discuss the wedding and, of course, the Marriage Settlement.'

*   *   *

Donela, having shut the Study door behind her, ran down the corridor and up the stairs.

She did not go to her mother's room as her step-father expected.

Instead, she went to her own.

She shut the door and pulled off her riding-habit and her boots.

Then she flung herself down on the bed to think.

How was it possible that, like a bolt out of the blue, she should be confronted with marriage.

It was only a week since she had returned to England.

It had been thrilling to come home.

She had also looked forward to having the Ball in London which her step-father had promised her.

She thought it would be fun to meet English girls of her own age.

Several of those who had been at School with her were to be presented this year.

Of course they had talked about who they would marry and hoped they would have lots of proposals.

"My sister had six proposals her first Season," one girl boasted, "and she married the seventh."

"Why was he any different from the others?" one of the French girls asked.

"He is the son of a Marquis!" the English girl replied.

There were no questions after that answer.

Donela knew it had been a social triumph which had delighted her whole family.

She thought now that, if she told the girls at School about Lord Waltingham, they would be impressed.

At the same time, she was sure that some of them would understand her reluctance to marrying a man so much older than herself.

"I said he was old enough to be my father," Donela mused, "but I could just as well have said my grandfather, because he seems so old."

Her father, perhaps because he was always at sea, had looked a young man when he died.

There had been no deep lines under his eyes, and he had not a grey hair on his head.

"I . . . cannot do it . . . I cannot!" Donela murmured.

It took her a long time to compose herself.

Finally, having changed into one of the pretty, expensive gowns her mother had sent her when she was in Florence, she left her bedroom.

Reluctantly she walked along the passage to her mother's *Boudoir*.

It was a lovely room adjoining Lady Grayson's bedroom.

It was where she sat in the mornings when she was dealing with household affairs.

She was studying the menu for the week-end when her daughter came into the room.

She looked up and knew exactly what she was feeling.

Just for a moment Donela stood inside the door, looking at her mother.

Then, as Lady Grayson rose to her feet, she rushed towards her and hid her face against her shoulder.

Her mother held her very close.

"I know, darling," she said in a gentle voice, "it has been a shock, but your step-father insisted on telling you the news himself."

"How can I . . . marry a . . . man who is so . . . old . . . older than Papa?" Donela asked.

Her mother did not answer, and after a moment she lifted her head to say:

"Do I . . . *have* to marry . . . him . . . Mama?"

Lady Grayson led her towards the sofa, and they sat down side by side.

"I was afraid, dearest," she said, "that this would upset you."

"I . . . I never thought . . . never dreamt I would be . . . pushed into marriage the . . . moment I arrived . . . back in England!" Donela said. "I was looking . . . forward to . . . being with you . . . in London . . . and the Balls . . . besides everything else that would be . . . fun . . . if you were . . . there."

"I know," Lady Grayson said with a note of pain in her voice. "But your step-father is so delighted at the idea of you marrying Lord Waltingham that there is nothing I can say."

"He wants to get rid of me!" Donela said defiantly.

"That is not the only reason," her mother answered. "Your step-father really believes that the luckiest thing that could happen to you would be to marry Lord Waltingham. He admires him so much, they were at School together, and have always been very close friends."

"But . . . Step-Papa is not marrying him!" Donela said bitterly. "I am."

"I wish I could help you, my darling," her mother said, "and I have suggested that you should wait until the Season was over in case you met anybody else whom you could love."

"And what did . . . my step-father say to . . . that?" Donela asked.

She knew the answer.

"He just got angry," Lady Grayson said in a very low voice.

Donela knew that her mother was a little afraid of Sir Marcus, not that he was ever angry with her.

But because she felt she owed him so much, she thought it was wrong for her to oppose him in any way.

"Surely, Mama," Donela said, "you can persuade Step-Papa that I should . . . wait at least . . . two months, or until the end of the Summer? Most girls have a long engagement."

Her mother did not answer and Donela went on:

"I suppose the truth is that . . . he is jealous of . . . me and wants . . . me out of the house . . . as quickly as . . . possible."

Her mother made a little smothered sound which told her she did not want to answer that question.

Donela moved from her mother's arms.

"Are you happy, Mama . . . really happy . . . as you were with . . . Papa?" she asked.

Her mother looked at her in surprise at the question.

Then her eyes flickered and she looked away.

There was an uncomfortable silence.

"It is all right, Mama," Donela said at length. "There is no reason for you to say anything. I know Papa would understand and not force me up the aisle with a man whom I dislike . . . and I think very soon . . . I shall . . . hate!"

"Oh, no, dearest, do not talk like that!" her mother begged.

"It is true, Mama. I thought yesterday when he was talking about himself at luncheon that he was a bore. Now, when I think of him as being my husband, I want to run away and hide!''

Lady Grayson clasped her hands together.

"Oh, darling, darling, what can I do? I cannot bear you to feel like this!''

Donela walked from the sofa across to the window.

Once again she was looking out, but she was not seeing the sunshine, the flowers, or the trees in the Park.

She was hearing her own voice saying:

"I want to run away and hide!''

It gave her an idea, an idea that was so stupendous that for a moment it was difficult to think what it implied.

With an effort she turned towards her mother.

Lady Grayson was looking very beautiful, but at the same time pale.

She was, too, very much thinner than when Donela went abroad.

"You are not to upset yourself, Mama,'' she said. "Somehow I will think out what I must do, and perhaps, whatever it is, Papa . . . will be . . . helping me.''

The tears came into Lady Grayson's eyes.

"I am sure, my dearest, he will do that. I know he is thinking of you, loving you, and he was always so very, very proud of you!''

"That is what I wanted you to say," Donela answered. "So, for the moment, Mama, we will leave it in Papa's hands. I am sure he will not fail me!''

"How could he do so when he loved you so much!'' her mother replied.

chapter two

DONELA spent the afternoon with her mother.

She thought Sir Marcus looked at her questioningly.

However, nothing further was said about Lord Waltingham.

But she was acutely conscious that the hours were passing.

Tomorrow he would arrive to propose to her, absolutely certain that she would accept.

'I have no . . . choice,' she thought bitterly.

Then the idea of running away was back in her mind.

When she went up to dress for dinner, she looked at her clothes.

She wondered what she should take with her.

It was not going to be easy.

She also had to decide for how long she would stay away.

The answer was as long as it took her step-father to accept her decision that she would not marry Lord Waltingham.

She did not imagine that Lord Waltingham would take her refusal easily.

He was obviously very puffed up with his own importance.

He would believe that any woman he asked to be his wife would jump at the opportunity.

Even to think of him made Donela shiver.

She knew, although it seemed an hysterical thing to say, that she would rather die than be married to him.

Then the common sense which she had inherited from her father told her there was no need for such dramatics.

She would merely go away and disappear for a short while.

When she returned, Sir Marcus would have taken her protestations seriously.

She knew she could not stay away for ever.

The simple reason for that was, it would be very difficult for her to earn her own living.

She knew that if she wished to be a Governess or a Companion, she would have to produce a reference.

If she faked one, she might be caught out.

Perhaps she would be arrested and charged with forgery.

All sorts of different ideas came into her mind to frighten her.

Yet she was still determined that whatever happened, she would not meet Lord Waltingham tomorrow.

Once again she went to the piano after dinner.

She did not play the light-hearted songs she had chosen the night before.

Instead, the Drawing-Room was filled with the sound of soft classical music by Chopin and Mozart.

Even so, she had the idea that Sir Marcus looked at her resentfully.

She was sure he thought the music was interrupting his conversation.

At ten o'clock Donela said goodnight and went upstairs.

She told the maid who looked after her not to wait up.

She managed to unbutton her own evening-gown.

As she hung it up she saw a carpet-bag at the bottom of the wardrobe.

It was one she had bought in Florence.

There had been no room in her trunk for all her books.

At the last moment she had bought the bag and filled it with them.

It was large and roomy, but at the same time it was light to carry.

Almost as if her father were guiding her, she knew this was her "luggage."

She chose which gown she would wear.

Although it was pretty, it was not so elaborate as to cause comment.

27

It had a short velvet jacket to wear over it and was a deep blue.

There was a smart little hat to match, which was a background for her beautiful hair.

That was one problem settled.

Now she had to think what she must pack.

Because she was going to be away in the Summer, she put two light muslin gowns in the bag.

She added another of white gauze that she could wear in the evening.

They took up relatively little space in the carpet-bag.

Even when she had slipped in two soft nightgowns and a muslin negligee there was room for a pair of slippers.

Also her hair-brush, comb, and a box of hairpins.

A number of extras like handkerchiefs, a sponge, and a toothbrush went on top.

She was sure that during the night she would think of other things which were absolutely necessary.

Now the problem was money.

She had little left over from the journey home.

Her step-father had sent her a generous cheque so that she could tip the servants at School and the porters on the Railway.

"I need much more," she told herself.

Then she remembered that her mother always had money in her handbag.

'I shall ask her for some early in the morning,' Donela decided.

As she undressed and got into bed she was thinking

that her step-father would be furious when he knew she had gone.

At the same time, she was sure her father would think she was doing the right thing.

"You must always follow your Star," he once said.

She had looked at him enquiringly, and he explained:

"When I am on the bridge at sea I look up at the sky and I feel there is one Star there guiding me, on which I can rely."

"And you think your Star tells you what to do, Papa?" Donela asked.

"I am sure the ideas that come into my mind are put there by someone cleverer than I am," the Captain replied.

It was something Donela had always remembered.

When she looked up at the sky she would wonder which, amongst the thousands of Stars twinkling overhead, was hers.

'I will follow my Star, Papa,' she said now in her heart, 'but you . . . must help . . . me too.'

*   *   *

Donela awoke early, before she was called.

She dressed herself carefully in her pretty gown.

She did not put on the jacket or the hat.

She waited until she heard Sir Marcus leave her mother's room and walk to his own.

He was an early riser.

She knew he would go to the stables either to ride

or to inspect the horses before breakfast.

She waited just in case he went back to see her mother before he went downstairs.

Then, when she knew he had gone, she went along the passage to her mother's room.

Lady Grayson was still in bed.

As her daughter came in she smiled with delight at seeing her.

"I am lazy, darling," she said, "but I have a slight headache, so I thought I would rest until luncheon-time."

"That is very sensible of you, Mama," Donela said, kissing her, "but the reason I have come is to ask you for some money."

"Some money?" Lady Grayson questioned.

"I want to go into the village to see if I can find myself a new riding-whip. If I cannot buy one there, I may have to go into St. Albans."

She paused, then before her mother could speak she said:

"I do not want to ask . . . Step-Papa for any-thing . . . more than he has . . . given me . . . already."

"No, of course not," her mother agreed. "You will find plenty of money in my handbag. Take what you want."

Donela went to the chest-of-drawers where she knew her mother's handbag was kept.

She opened it and found there was even more money than she had expected.

She did not say anything, but took nearly all of it.

"Thank you, Mama," she said as she slipped it into her pocket.

She went back to the bed-side and kissed her mother affectionately.

"You must take care of yourself, Mama," she said, "and not do too much."

"I will try not to," Lady Grayson replied, "but you know your step-father does not like doing anything without me, and we have had quite a number of long drives recently which I do find exhausting."

Donela kissed her again.

"I love you, Mama!" she said.

"And I love you, my darling," her mother replied.

She seemed about to say something else, then changed her mind as if she thought it would be a mistake.

Because she had no wish to discuss Lord Waltingham in any way, Donela hurried away.

Only when she reached her own room did she wipe the tears from her eyes.

It was very hard to leave her mother after she had been so long away from her.

"Mama will be upset," she told herself.

Then she thought if nothing else, it might make Sir Marcus think again.

She had already written the letter she was leaving behind.

It was in her handbag in which she now placed the money she had taken from her mother.

Putting on her hat and the little velvet jacket, she picked up the carpet-bag.

She went along the corridor and down the secondary staircase, which was the nearest to the stables.

She was praying as she went that Sir Marcus would have gone riding.

She did not want him to ask questions about where she was going.

Her prayers were answered.

As she emerged from the path which led from the house to the stable-yard she saw him in the far distance.

He was riding towards the flatland, where he could gallop.

She ordered the pony-trap, which was what her mother always used for short journeys.

The pony that drew it was actually a small horse, young and quite fast.

He was led from his stall and put between the shafts.

Donela said she would like to take Ben with her.

Ben was one of the younger grooms, who had been there before she went abroad.

He was, she was convinced, one of the most stupid.

He was good with horses, but he found it very difficult to talk to people.

They therefore drove to the village in silence.

Donela had no intention of stopping at the few shops which provided everything.

She went on until she had reached the main road which ran through the Hertfordshire countryside.

At the first cross-roads she drew the pony and trap to a standstill and said to Ben:

"I am being collected here by some friends. There is no need for you to wait. Go back to the house and when you get there hand in this note and say it is to be taken up to Her Ladyship.''

Ben showed no surprise at this strange order.

He took the note and thrust it into the pocket of his coat.

Donela handed him the reins and he turned the horse round.

He did not say goodbye, but merely touched his forelock.

Donela raised her hand.

She watched the pony and trap until it was out of sight.

Then she looked up and down the road, waiting for a Stage-Coach.

She was certain one would come from one direction or the other.

She had no particular desire to go in either, preferring to leave the decision to fate.

If the coach was going to London, that was the way she would travel.

If it was approaching from the other direction, then she would believe that was the way chosen by her Star.

The only thing that worried her was that perhaps the Stage-Coach had already passed this particular point.

If she had to wait for a long time, her step-father might come in search of her.

She had just begun to pray that this would not happen.

Then she saw in the distance a cloud of dust coming from the direction of London.

It was only a few seconds later that she knew it was a Stage-Coach approaching.

She had been afraid it might be some other traveller.

It came nearer and nearer.

It was a new, well-painted vehicle drawn by four horses.

Because it was a fine day and the sun was shining, there were quite a number of men travelling on the roof.

This meant, Donela told herself hopefully, that there would be plenty of room inside.

She waved as the coach drew nearer.

The driver drew his horses up level with her.

The Guard, carrying his long brass horn, got down to open the door of the carriage.

"Ye've no luggage, Ma'am?" he asked politely.

"This is all I have," Donela answered, holding up her carpet-bag.

He took it from her and pushed it into the rack which was above the back seat.

Then he stood to one side to allow Donela to enter the coach.

She saw with relief that it was not over-crowded.

There was an old woman who looked like a Farmer's wife sitting in one corner.

She had a basket beside her in which there were eggs and two plucked chickens.

In the other corner, facing her, there were two extremely pretty, if flashily dressed, young girls.

Beside them was a man who also seemed to be too smartly dressed for the country.

When he realised that, as the seat was full, Donela would have to sit with her back to the horses, he said:

"Allow me, Ma'am, to give you my seat, where I know you'll be more comfortable."

"That is very kind of you," Donela exclaimed.

The man moved over, and as he did so the Guard asked:

"Now then, Ma'am, where might ye be a-goin'?"

Donela had almost forgotten that she would have to pay her fare.

"I am not certain," she answered. "What is your final destination?"

"Last stop afore Oxford be Little Fording," the Guard replied.

Donela hesitated.

She thought it might be rather frightening to arrive in Oxford late in the day.

She would not know where to go, or where she should stay.

"Little Fording's where we're goin'," one of the girls beside her said. "I hears it's ever so pretty!"

"Then that is where I will go," Donela said.

The Guard, impatient to be off, asked her for three-shillings, which she gave him.

He slammed the door and climbed up on the box beside the coach-driver.

As they moved off he blew on his horn.

Donela settled herself a little more comfortably in the corner seat.

She was aware that the man opposite her was staring at her in undisguised admiration.

Now that she could examine him more closely, she

realised he was, in fact, very over-dressed.

He was wearing a close-fitting coat which accentuated his shoulders and which she thought must be padded.

He had a tie-pin which glinted in the sunlight coming through the windows.

There was a yellow carnation in his buttonhole.

His trousers were of a loud check.

The top hat which was next to her carpet-bag above her head belonged to him.

"We've a long journey before us," he said conversationally.

"What time do you expect to arrive?" Donela asked.

"In time for us t'dress," one of the girls on the other side of her replied, "and that takes a long time, I can tell you."

Donela looked at her in surprise.

Then she thought from the way both the young women were turned out, it would obviously take both time and effort.

Their hats were decorated with feathers.

Their gowns were in bright colours, one being a strong shade of pink, the other a bright blue.

There was lace round the neck and the sleeves, satin sashes, and a profusion of frills at the hems of their skirts.

As if the girl could read her thoughts and knew she was wondering what they could be, she said with a giggle:

"That's right! We come from London an' we don't fit in wiv all the hedges and turnips!"

She made it sound so funny that Donela could not help laughing.

The man opposite her intervened:

"I think, Ma'am, we should introduce ourselves," he said. "I don't suppose you've heard of me, but the name's Basil Banks."

"I am afraid not," Donela replied, "but I have only just come back to England, having been abroad for over a year."

"Well, that would account for it!" he said. "But all the most important people in London have heard of '*Basil Banks and his Three Belles*.'"

"Only two today," the girl next to Donela corrected him.

"As you so rightly say," Basil Banks agreed, "only two. And I only hopes His Lordship don't cut up rough."

"If he do, there ain't nothing we can do about it," the girl said. "Milly woulda been useless what with that temperature and coughing her heart out!"

Donela looked bewildered and Mr. Banks explained:

"Milly's my third 'Belle,' and when we went to pick her up this morning she was really bad, so we just had to leave her behind."

"What are you going to do?" Donela asked.

"We're a Song an' Dance Act," Mr. Banks explained, "and we're a great draw, I can tell you, at Evans's Supper Rooms!"

He saw that Donela had never heard of the place, and he drew from his pocket a leaflet which he handed to her as he explained:

"This'll show you where we've been performing for over a month. If you're ever in London, I know you'd enjoy not only the food, but also the entertainment."

"He's right," the girl beside Donela chimed in. "Everyone says it's the best Supper Rooms in Town, an' we're the best Act in the whole of Covent Garden!"

Basil Banks smiled.

"That's true enough," he said proudly, "and that's Kitty whose applause nearly takes the roof off, and on the other side of her—that's Daisy."

Donela smiled at them both.

Then Mr. Banks asked:

"And might we have the honour to know to whom we're speaking?"

"Yes, of course," Donela replied. "My name is Donela Colwyn."

Even as she spoke she wondered if it was a mistake to give her real name.

Then she told herself it was unlikely that her stepfather would expect her to be on the Stage-Coach.

If he did make enquiries, the Guard had no knowledge of who she was.

Doubtless after their performance Mr. Banks and his Belles would go back to London.

She looked at the leaflet Mr. Banks had passed to her and read:

EVANS'S SUPPER ROOMS
COVENT GARDEN

. . . . .

SELECTIONS
and words of
MADRIGALS, GLEES, CHORUSES
SONGS etc
SUNG EVERY EVENING
IN THE ABOVE SUPPER ROOMS
COMMENCING AT EIGHT PRECISELY
VOCALISTS
SOPRANI
VARIETY
BASIL BANKS AND HIS THREE BELLES

When she gave it back to him she said:

"It all sounds very exciting. I wish I could watch you perform."

"I wish you could too," Mr. Banks said. "It's a pity you're not a guest of His Lordship."

"Who is that?" Donela asked.

She had a sudden fear that by some quirk of fate, although it was very unlikely, he would say it was Lord Waltingham.

It was quite a relief when he replied:

"The Earl of Huntingford."

Donela had never heard of him.

Because she was relieved that it was not Lord Waltingham, she asked:

"Is he very important?"

Basil Banks smiled.

" 'Is Lordship's having a Point-to-Point today on

his estate, and tonight he's giving a big Dinner Party at which we're the main attraction!"

Donela thought it rather strange, but she was interested.

"Do you perform in the Dining-Room?" she asked, "or does he have a special Theatre?"

"I expect, in fact I'm sure," Basil Banks replied, "it'll be in the Dining-Room. Some gentlemen erect a small stage at the end and make it pretty with pots of flowers, while at others we just come onto the floor, so to speak."

"Is it difficult," Donela asked, "giving a performance for such a small audience?"

"Oh, there's no difficulty," Basil Banks said loftily. "We've appeared in all sorts of houses at one time or another, but the Earl of Huntingford's something special."

"Why is that?" Donela asked.

"You've never heard of him?"

Donela shook her head.

"Well, he's got some very fine horses. He's won the Derby and the Gold Cup at Ascot, and I made quite a bit of money!"

"That's better than losing," Kitty chimed in, "especially when you're starving because you're hard up!"

"Now, that's an unfair thing to say . . ." Basil Banks began.

Then he realised she was teasing him and said:

"Now, you shut up! I'm telling this lady about the Earl, and it's a pity she can't see him."

"Let's take her with us," Daisy suggested. "You

can always say she's the third 'Belle'!''

Basil Banks stared at Daisy before he exclaimed:

"That's not a bad idea! But I don't suppose Miss Colwyn will think it much of a compliment."

"I don't see why not," Kitty objected. "She's not the snooty kind who'd look down her nose at us."

She turned towards Donela.

"Now, are you, dearie?"

"I hope not," Donela said, "but I am not quite certain what you mean by 'the snooty kind.'"

"I'll tell you," Kitty said. "When we goes to some places to do our 'turn,' even though there's no Ladies there, the Housekeeper, the Cook, an' all the other servants behaves as if we're dirt under their feet!"

Donela thought she could understand that.

She knew how straitlaced and puritanical the old servants were in her step-father's house.

They would look at the rouge and lip-salve on Kitty and Daisy's lips and say they were "no better than they ought to be."

She realised Kitty was waiting for her to answer, and she said after a moment:

"I am afraid in quite a number of countries people are shocked by actresses."

"That's true enough," Basil Banks agreed. "But I always says, 'It takes all kinds to make a world,' and we has to 'live and let live.'"

"I am sure you are right," Donela replied, "and my father, who was a sailor, was never critical as some English people can be about foreigners."

She smiled before she continued:

"He used to say: 'They have their customs and we

41

have ours and we should respect rather than ridicule anything they do.' "

Basil Banks clapped his hands.

"That's right!" he said. "And I'm sure, Miss Colwyn, you don't think we're 'beyond the pale,' but human beings like anybody else."

"Of course I think that," Donela said as she smiled, "and I think it is very clever of you to be such a success that people applaud you and the Earl wants you to entertain his guests."

"That's what I likes to hear," Basil Banks approved. "Don't you, girls?"

" 'Corse we do!" Kitty and Daisy said in unison. "And as we're giving out compliments, I'd like to say that I think Miss Colwyn's real pretty. I've never seen such lovely hair before!"

"Thank you!" Donela said.

"If she's going to Little Fording with us," Daisy put in, "I can't see why she can't come to the house and watch us do our 'turn' from the side. After all, His Lordship's expecting you to bring three of us with you!"

She spoke as if she were working it out while she was talking.

Basil Banks threw out his hands.

"There you are—you're a success with my girls!" he said to Donela. "They want you to see how clever they are."

Donela would have murmured something, but he went on:

"But I expect, when you get to Little Fording you've got friends waiting for you."

"As a matter of fact I have never heard of the village until you said you were going there," Donela answered, "and perhaps you can tell me if there is a quiet Inn where I could stay for the night?"

Basil Banks stared at her.

"Are you saying you're on your own, with no one looking after you?"

"I am afraid that is the truth," Donela replied, "but I shall be all right."

"You'd better be careful!" Kitty warned. "You never knows what you'll find in these outlandish places! It's bad enough in London, but it's so quiet in the country, it fair gives me the creeps!"

Basil Banks was looking at Donela.

"You're very beautiful, Miss Colwyn," he said after a moment, "and it's strange for a beautiful woman to be wandering about on her own."

Donela suddenly felt a little frightened.

It had seemed so easy to run away.

She had not really thought of the strangers she would encounter.

They might be familiar if she was unchaperoned and wandering about on her own.

"I . . . I am sure I shall be . . . all right," she said bravely. "In the village where I lived in Worcester-shire, there was a very nice Inn kept by an elderly couple who would not allow any rowdyism in the place."

"You might be lucky—you might not," Basil Banks said. "I went into an Inn in a village the other day. I've never seen such goings-on! Drunk as Lords, they all were, and stealing from each other. I got out far quicker than I went in!''

Donela's eyes widened.

She had never thought anything like that could happen.

She had imagined she would find a place like The Green Dragon.

Old Mr. Hitchin had been respectful to her when she was a child.

His wife would often give her a jar of home-made pickles to take back to her mother.

Then she consoled herself with the thought that if Little Fording was noisy and unpleasant, she would go somewhere else.

She looked at Basil Banks and realised he had been watching her.

He must have guessed what she was thinking.

He bent forward.

''If you're really alone, Miss Colwyn,'' he said, ''why don't you come with us? We're only staying for one night, then going back to London tomorrow morning. No one'll ask questions if I arrive, as expected, with three girls.''

''If you arrive with two,'' Kitty remarked, ''you'll have to explain why Milly ain't with us. They always says at Evans's that His Lordship expects to get what he wants, and be very disagreeable if he don't.''

''I've heard that too,'' Basil Banks said, ''but His Lordship has always behaved like a gentleman to me!''

''There's always a first time!'' Daisy warned.

''All right, all right!'' Basil Banks said. ''And what

it comes down to, Miss Colwyn, is that I'd be mighty obliged if you'd come with us and prevent me from having to answer some uncomfortable questions."

"I really do not see why His Lordship should blame you for one of your girls being sick," Donela said nervously.

Basil Banks gave a short laugh.

"You don't know what these titled folk are like!" he said. "They expect to get what they pay for, and don't listen to no excuses!"

"I think that is unfair!" Donela said.

"There's no question of 'fair' when you're working for money. You either 'deliver the goods,' or you don't get paid!"

"Are you really suggesting that the Earl of Huntingford would refuse to pay you what he promised if one of your girls was too ill to perform?" Donela asked.

"He might and he might not," Basil Banks answered. "He certainly won't be pleased when he's got everything planned, then finds himself short-handed, so to speak."

"Oh, come on!" Kitty pleaded. "Be a sport and come with us! You're ever so pretty, and in Milly's get-up no-one will guess it's not her. Why should they?"

"That's true enough," Basil Banks agreed. "And I think I should explain, Miss Colwyn, that my three girls wear wigs so they really do look alike."

He smiled before he added:

"I thought when I was planning the Act I'd call it *'Basil Banks and the Three Sisters,'* then someone suggested 'Belles' would fit in better with my name."

"Are you saying that your girls are all dressed alike?" Donela asked.

"Oh, they have several changes," Basil Banks replied. "I don't suppose, by any lucky chance, you can sing?"

Donela hesitated.

"I have had singing lessons," she said, "and the other girls at School and I had competitions."

"What sort?" Basil Banks asked.

Donela explained how they played and sang the popular songs from their own countries and how last year she had won the prize because her mother had sent her the most popular songs from the Music Halls.

"I don't believe it!" he said. "It's too good to be true! Now, just you tell me, Miss Colwyn, what you sang to them?"

Donela told him how she had sung "Champagne Charlie" and "Gilbert the Filbert," but the one they liked best was "A Voice from the Dark."

"Well, all I can say is the gods are on my side!" Basil Banks exclaimed. "With your looks and wearing Milly's costume you'll bring the house down!"

"You have not heard me yet!" Donela answered.

"I'm just betting on a certainty you'll be a 'smash hit'!"

" 'Corse she will," Kitty joined in. "And she's ever so pretty—far prettier than Milly!"

"I can see that," Basil Banks replied, "but she'll have to be kind enough to let us put on some make-up. The gentlemen'll feel uncomfortable if they thinks there's a Lady present!"

There was a little pause before Donela asked:

"But . . . why should it make them . . . uncomfortable?"

"Because it's a 'Stag-Party'—gentlemen only, Miss Colwyn," Basil Banks replied, "and gentlemen, especially after they've been riding all day, likes to let themselves go when there's no disapproving mothers or wives around to tell them to behave themselves!"

"You mean . . . the Earl has a party for . . . men only?" Donela asked, trying to understand.

Mr. Banks hesitated, then he said:

"Of course, sometimes on these occasions the gentlemen guests bring their own lady-friends."

He spoke a little awkwardly, as if he did not wish to explain any further.

Donela did not like to press him.

It seemed strange.

But all she was thinking was, if she did go with these nice people, at least she would not have to worry where she should stay tonight.

Finding a room for herself in a strange village where she knew no one might be difficult.

She knew now that, in running away, she had not thought it out properly.

Nor had she considered what she would do with herself once she was in hiding.

If she agreed to Mr. Banks's proposition to stay with the Earl, at least she could start tomorrow morning, considering her position.

She would also have time to decide where she might go next.

47

"I will go to the village and have a look at it," she told herself. "Then if the Inn seems dirty and likely to have rowdy customers in it, I can move on to Oxford, or perhaps another village, where things are better."

It was all rather vague in her mind.

At the same time, although she did not like to admit it, she felt frightened.

It had all seemed so easy last night to slip away to make Sir Marcus understand he could not push her into matrimony.

Now it appeared there might be other problems.

In fact, ones which could frighten her nearly as much as Lord Waltingham.

She made up her mind.

"If you really want me," she said, "and you are certain I shall not be an encumbrance, I would love to come with you."

"We want you all right," Basil Banks said. "In fact, to tell you the truth, I'm really grateful to you for getting me out of a hole."

"I want you to see Daisy and me perform," Kitty added. "Everyone says we're sensational, but we've never had a Lady on the show with us before."

"We haven't," Daisy piped up, "and we can tell you're a Lady, even if His Lordship mustn't find out about it."

"That's true," Basil Banks said in a serious tone, "and we must be certain we make no mistakes."

"It's a mistake, for one thing," Kitty said, "for you to go on callin' her 'Miss Colwyn.'"

"You're right," Basil Banks agreed.

He looked across the carriage at Donela.

"Do you mind if I call you Donela? It's a pretty name, and even sounds theatrical."

"Of course I do not mind," Donela said, "and I agree with you that it would be a mistake for the Earl to think I am anything but what I am supposed to be."

"Well, I'm not going to ask of you anything you can't do," Basil Banks said. "If we get there at four o'clock, there'll be plenty of time for me to run through your song and that will be your 'turn.' Otherwise you just have to look pretty and more or less keep in the background."

"That is what I want to do," Donela said.

She could not help worrying.

Perhaps, when Basil Banks heard her sing, he would think her voice was not good enough.

Then she remembered that everybody in the School had said she had a good voice.

Because she was in the Choir, she was occasionally given a small solo part in the Chapel Services.

'I shall be all right,' she thought. 'After all, I am only singing in a Dining-Room, so it cannot be too big.'

She must have shown what she was thinking, because Basil Banks bent forward to say:

"Now, don't you worry yourself, Donela. You'll be marvellous, and we'll take very good care of you, won't we, girls?"

" 'Corse we will," Kitty agreed. "I don't like to think of you sleepin' all alone in some terrible old Inn where there might be ghosts!"

Daisy laughed.

"More likely human ones knocking on her door!"

Once again Donela shivered.

"If everything is going to be difficult," she told herself, "I shall have to go home. Perhaps even Lord Waltingham will not be as bad as some drunken reveller who insults me because I am alone."

Kitty was already talking excitedly about what she was to wear.

"Our wigs are ever so pretty!" she said. "All golden, like your hair, only without the red in it, and curly. We always gets a round of applause when we comes on."

"That's true," Basil Banks said as he smiled. "It was my idea to have them all looking alike. Someone's bound to copy the idea sooner or later, but for the moment, we're unique."

"We are that," Daisy said, "and we've got a very unique thing up our sleeve, as you well knows!"

"Well, it's no use upsetting Donela," Basil Banks said sharply.

Donela did not understand why she should be upset.

But he quickly changed the subject.

Then she told herself the only thing that mattered was that she was lucky for tonight, at any rate.

Her mother would not approve of her new friends, but her father would understand.

chapter three

THE Stage-Coach stopped at a Posting Inn for luncheon.

Basil Banks managed to get a table for the four of them.

They did not have to sit with the rather rowdy men who had been on top of the coach.

They, however, made up to Kitty and Daisy, asking them why they did not come and sit on top with them.

"I don't trust you not to push me over the side!" Kitty replied.

She was laughing as she spoke and looked so pretty that Donela could understand when the man said:

"Aw, come on! You needn't be afraid, I'll hold yer tight."

"That's what I am afraid of!" Kitty retorted pertly, and the other men laughed.

51

Donela knew her mother would have been shocked, but she thought it was all just good-humoured, light-hearted chaff.

She was also sure that Basil Banks would look after his girls if there was any trouble.

He gave himself airs and did not exchange jokes with the other men.

He obviously thought them beneath him.

He certainly looked very smart compared to them.

When he put his top-hat on at an angle, he looked somewhat odd in the countryside.

The luncheon that was provided for the travellers was not very good.

There was, however, plenty of bread and cheese if they were hungry, and the men all drank ale.

The Driver and the Guard were obviously in a hurry to be on their way.

They set off again, the horses being urged to go swiftly despite the fact that the Stage-Coach must have been very heavy.

Donela remembered her father telling her that the coaches were often over-loaded.

This meant that the life of the horses that drew them was not more than three years.

She did not like to think about it, knowing how much she enjoyed riding the superb horses that belonged to her step-father.

They were looked after by the grooms as if they were Royalty.

As soon as the travellers were back in the coach, Basil Banks settled himself comfortably in the corner and closed his eyes.

He was obviously sleepy after several glasses of ale.

Donela thought she would be wise to try to sleep too.

She had been so worried last night that she had lain awake tossing and turning.

If she had to perform tonight in front of the Earl and his friends, she would need all her wits about her.

It was, however, difficult to sleep.

While Kitty and Daisy dozed, Donela found herself thinking that this was a very unusual adventure.

How could she have imagined, when she had decided to run away by Stage-Coach, that she would find herself with a Variety Turn from London.

What was more, they had persuaded her to join them for the night.

"I am sure Papa would think it very amusing," she told herself.

At the same time, her conscience was pricking her.

She knew as a Lady it was certainly something she should not do.

"But what is the point of being a Lady if it means being pushed into marriage with an old man one dislikes," she argued.

There was no answer to that.

So she sat listening to the wheels turning beneath her and the sound of the horses' hoofs.

They arrived in the village of Little Fording later than they had expected.

As they drove through it, Donela could understand why Kitty had said it was pretty.

All the cottages were painted white and had thatched roofs.

The window frames and door were bright blue and the gardens were a blaze of colour.

With daffodils and tulips growing in them, she thought the whole place looked very picturesque.

They crossed the ford from which the village had got its name.

As they proceeded farther, the cottages were only on one side of the road.

On the other there was a high brick wall.

Donela guessed without being told that it surrounded the Earl's Estate.

She knew she was not mistaken when a little farther on they came to a pair of magnificent wrought-iron gates tipped with gold.

There were two lodges, one on each side of them.

Their doors and shutters were painted in the same blue as the cottages.

The Stage-Coach drew to a standstill outside the gates.

The girls had put on their hats which they had taken off while they dozed, and Kitty said excitedly:

"Here we are! I hopes there's a carriage waiting for us!"

"I'm far too tired to walk," Daisy said plaintively.

"Don't worry," Basil Banks said. "If His Lordship said there's be a carriage, then there'll be one!"

The Guard climbed down to open the door.

As they stepped out, Donela could see there was a smart carriage drawn up just inside the gates.

A footman in a smart livery and a cockaded hat came hurrying towards them.

Basil Banks said:

"I'm Mr. Banks, and I expect you've been sent by the Earl of Huntingford to meet us."

The footman touched his hat.

"That's right, Sir. I expects you have some luggage."

"Quite a lot of it," Basil Banks replied.

The Guard was already unstrapping several large trunks from the back of the coach.

It was obvious that the footman could not manage them alone.

He spoke to one of the villagers who was standing staring at the coach as if he knew there would be someone unusual in it.

Certainly, when Kitty and Daisy appeared, women came out from their cottages.

They leant over the gates to stare.

Picking up their skirts to avoid the dust, Kitty and Daisy walked elegantly towards the carriage.

The footman ran to open the door for them.

The carriage was open.

As Donela joined them, she thought that everything that was happening might be on a stage.

It certainly did not seem real: the huge Gates, the high brick wall, the carriage drawn by what she realised were outstanding horses.

Daisy and Kitty, looking like two brilliantly winged parakeets, waited for Basil Banks to join them.

All the luggage, and there really was a lot of it, was removed from the Stage-Coach.

The Guard then quickly climbed up onto the box and blew his horn as if in farewell.

The horses moved off and the men on top waved to Kitty and Daisy.

As they did so they shouted:

"Now you're so posh," one said, "don't forget us!"

"I won't!" Kitty shouted back.

There were cheers and some of the men waved their hats as they drove away.

Kitty, who had stood up in the carriage to see them go, resumed her seat.

"They were a cheery lot!" she remarked. "I only hopes them 'toffs' watching us tonight'll be half so enthusiastic!"

"And generous with their money!" Daisy said. "I don't suppose His Lordship's stingy when it comes to his own comfort."

Basil Banks came hurrying up to the carriage.

"The luggage is being fetched by a Brake," he said as he climbed into it. "The footman says it won't be long and it'll be with us by the time we've had a cup of tea."

"That's what I'm longing for!" Kitty said. "My throat's dry as a hayrick!"

Daisy also said she was longing for a drink.

Donela, however, was not listening.

They had moved through the gates, and she wanted to see what sort of house the Earl of Huntingford possessed.

She wondered if it would be as large as her step-father's.

If the Earl belonged to an ancient family, it would be old.

The drive was a long one, lined on either side by ancient oak trees.

Then, as it curved slightly, she had her first glimpse of the Earl's house and was exceedingly impressed.

It was built on higher ground against a background of fir trees.

It was, she knew, of the Georgian period and had doubtless been designed about 1750.

Her mother had taught her a great deal about architecture.

She realised as they drew nearer that the Earl of Huntingford's home was not only extremely impressive but also very beautiful.

There was a green lawn sloping down to an oval-shaped lake which was spanned by an ancient stone bridge.

The gardens that surrounded the house were brilliant with blossom.

There were almond trees, pink and white, and several large magnolias just coming into bloom.

The sun was shining on the windows, making them gleam like jewels.

Silhouetted against the sky there were urns and statues besides the Earl's standard which was flying in the breeze.

It was all so lovely that Donela felt her heart leap with excitement.

This was how she had always thought of England when she was living abroad.

This was the England she had always admired and to which she was proud to belong.

"Coo-er!" Kitty exclaimed as they crossed over the bridge. "His Nibs don't half live in style!"

"I told you he was important," Basil Banks said, "and it's a compliment I appreciate being asked to come down here and entertain his guests."

"It were a long way," Daisy remarked, "and I only hopes he makes it worth our while."

"You can leave all that to me," Basil Banks said, "and mind you girls make yourselves pleasant to everybody. You'll be with *gentlemen* tonight, not those 'riff-raff' that sometimes come to Evans's, even if it is the smartest place in Town!"

For once Kitty had no answer ready because she was staring awe-struck at the house ahead.

The carriage approached the front-door.

Donela could see there was a white-haired Butler waiting for them.

There was, however, no red carpet laid down the steps.

She knew it would have been there had they been distinguished visitors and not mere entertainers.

She thought as she got out of the carriage that it was amusing to note the difference.

"Good-afternoon, Mr. Banks," the Butler said. "His Lordship will be delighted to know you have arrived. A footman will show you to your rooms and the Housekeeper will be waiting to attend to the young women."

Donela noted that he did not say "Ladies."

The footman started walking ahead, and they followed him down the passage.

They came to a second staircase which was by no means as impressive as the one leading from the hall.

They followed him up it.

At the top, waiting for them, was the Housekeeper in rustling black with a silver chatelaine at her waist.

Basil Banks, who had walked just behind the footman, greeted her.

"Good-afternoon," he said, "I understand you are going to show my young ladies to their bedrooms, and after that I would be obliged if I could see the room in which we are to perform this evening."

"It has all been arranged," the Housekeeper replied in a cold voice, "and on His Lordship's instructions, we have prepared four bedrooms and a Sitting-Room, where there is a piano."

She spoke the last word as if she were referring to something unpleasant.

But Basil Banks exclaimed:

"That's excellent, and extremely thoughtful of His Lordship."

He glanced at Donela as he spoke.

She knew he was thinking that he would be able to rehearse her song.

The bedrooms were in a side wing and not the centre of the house.

They were well furnished and, Donela thought, very comfortable.

They all opened onto one long corridor.

She gathered that Mr. Banks was on the other side of it, a little way from them.

The Sitting-Room was much nearer.

She saw Mr. Banks go into it as the Housekeeper showed Donela her room.

"One of the housemaids will help you with anything you want unpacked," the Housekeeper told her in a cold and lofty voice. "Tea has been provided for you in the Sitting-Room."

She did not wait for an answer.

She swept away as if she had condescended quite long enough to talk to people she considered were very much beneath her.

Donela could not help laughing, thinking it was very funny.

It was exactly how she would expect the servants to behave in her step-father's house.

She walked across the room to the window to look out onto the garden.

There was a fountain throwing its water into the air.

Directly below the window was a rose-garden planted round an ancient sun-dial.

'It is lovely!' she thought. 'And certainly no one will find me here.'

It seemed rather a joke that by this time her step-father would be looking for her.

It would never enter his mind that she was staying in the house of an Earl.

She took off her hat and her little velvet jacket.

She was just about to go into the Sitting-Room when Kitty came into her room.

"Basil's just remembered," she said, "that we never made you up before you come into the house!"

Donela looked at her in surprise.

"Made me up?" she exclaimed.

"Well, you can't be one of us looking as you do now!" Kitty said.

She walked across to the dressing-table and put a box down on it.

"Come on," she said, "I'll put a bit of rouge on your cheeks and some salve on your lips, then later we'll do your eyes."

It had never occurred to Donela that she might have to be made up before the evening.

Now she was aware that if they encountered the Earl or anyone who was observant, she looked very different from Kitty and Daisy.

She therefore sat down in front of the mirror.

Kitty skilfully rouged her cheeks, powdered her face, then made up her lips.

When she had finished, Donela looked at her reflection and laughed.

"I do look different!" she exclaimed.

"You looks very pretty!" Kitty said. "An' remember—you're a *Belle* and no one must know any different."

"No, of course not," Donela agreed. "I was thinking how lucky I was to be in this beautiful house tonight instead of in some small, uncomfortable Inn."

"I can't think what you're doing, wandering about all on your own!" Kitty said. "I ain't asking no questions, but I'm not pretending I'm not curious!"

"Perhaps I will tell you about it another time," Donela said quickly. "Now I am longing for a cup of tea."

"So am I!" Kitty agreed. "I could also do with something to eat."

They walked across the passage to the Sitting-Room.

Basil Banks was at the piano.

He was running his fingers over the keys.

Donela realised he was an accomplished player.

Kitty, however, had gone to a table in the centre of the room on which was laid out a very substantial tea.

There were cucumber sandwiches, hot scones in a covered dish, several sorts of cake, as well as a plate of chocolate biscuits.

"Now, that's what I calls a tea!" Kitty exclaimed. "Three cheers for His Lordship, and let's hope we goes home with our pockets full of money!"

Donela looked at her in surprise.

Before she could ask why Kitty should expect to receive any money from the Earl or his friends, Basil Banks rose from the piano.

"We don't want that sort of talk here," he said sharply. "You never know who's listening. Sit down and eat. When the luggage arrives, we have a lot of work to do."

Even as he spoke, the door opened and Daisy came in to say:

"The luggage is here and I've told them what rooms to put the trunks in. Milly's clothes have gone into Donela's room."

"I should have done that!" Basil Banks said.

He went out of the room, shutting the door behind him.

The three girls sat down at the table.

"If I eats all this," Daisy remarked, "I'll never get my corset laced!"

"That's true," Kitty replied, "but it's best to eat now, 'cause we probably won't eat much supper tonight, if we gets any at all!"

She saw Donela look at her questioningly, and she said:

"We does our turn while the gentry drinks themselves silly. Then when we join them we have something t'eat, if we're lucky!"

"We *join* them?" Donela questioned.

" 'Corse we do," Daisy said, "and I can tell you, I wants some champagne after all that exercise."

Donela did not understand.

She did not have time to ask questions because Basil Banks came back into the room.

"The first thing I want you girls to do," he said, "is to try Milly's gown on Donela and see that it fits. It looks as if it will, but you can never be sure."

"I'm having me tea first," Kitty replied, "and if Donela's only going to sing, we won't have to worry about her bursting at the seams!"

"That's true," Basil Banks agreed, pouring himself out a cup of tea, "but she has to look glamorous, and one of you should have remembered to make her up before we came into the house."

"It's all right," Kitty said. "Nobody noticed. And she's pretty enough to get away with anything!"

"That's not the point," Basil Banks said sharply. "She's got to look like a '*Belle*' and it's up to you to see that she does. For God's sake, put your wigs on properly. Daisy's nearly came off the other night!''

"It wasn't my fault!" Daisy whined. "And it slipped only a little."

"It made you look like a clown!" Basil Banks said. "We don't want any mistakes this evening, and that's for sure!"

"Oh, shut up!" Kitty said. "There's going to be no mistakes, and you're only in a tizzy 'cause of the High and Mighty Earl. He's only human, like the rest of us."

There was something so funny in the way she spoke that Basil Banks laughed.

"That's true," he said, "and after all, it's only a 'one-night stand.' If they don't like us, who cares!"

"That's what I thinks," Kitty said, "but you can bet your damned life they're going to like us, and Donela'll be a smash hit—just you wait and see!"

Donela was listening in astonishment.

She could not understand what all this was about.

She was surprised at Kitty swearing even though she was an actress.

Anyway, she wanted everything to go smoothly because Mr. Banks had been so kind to her.

She therefore hurried over her tea, and when he went to the piano she joined him.

He played several chords, then started a chorus of "A Voice in the Dark."

The two girls had left the room, and Donela sang quietly and naturally without feeling nervous.

As she finished the last line, Basil Banks lifted his hands from the keyboard and exclaimed:

"Perfect! Exactly how I thought you would sing!

64

It will certainly surprise those listening."

"Do you really mean that?" Donela asked.

"Your voice is quite different from what they'll expect," he said. "There's no need for any more rehearsing. Just sing tonight as you did just now, and when they applaud you, curtsy."

"I will do that," Donela said, "and perhaps I had better see to my clothes."

"I'm going to my room," Basil Banks said.

She thought as she went to her bedroom that it was rather strange that he did not want her to rehearse any further.

But at least she did not have to worry that she was not good enough.

Milly's trunk was a large one.

The straps had been undone by the footman who had carried it up the stairs.

Kitty came from her room to take out a large "Picture Dress" in which, she explained, Milly had appeared to sing one of her songs.

"What was it?" Donela asked.

There was a little pause before Kitty said:

"It wasn't a song that'd be suitable for you!"

"Why not?" Donela enquired.

"It's entitled 'Won't You Play with Me?' " Kitty answered, "and you're too much of a Lady to put it over."

Donela thought that was a funny thing to say.

Kitty was getting the wig out of the trunk, and she looked at it with interest.

It travelled in a special box, and she saw that it

was packed so that it would not be crushed in any way.

The hair was fair and shining, almost as if paint had been added to some of the curls.

Donela could imagine that, with three of them all looking the same, it would be very effective.

"You can try that on in a minute," Kitty said, "and if you ask me, instead of fussing over the gown, which I knows will fit you, you should be having a rest."

"Is that what you are going to do?" Donela enquired.

"You can bet your life I am!" Kitty replied. "I didn't get to sleep 'til four o'clock this morning, and we had to be up by seven."

"What made you so late?" Donela asked.

Kitty did not answer.

She was searching in the trunk for the shoes that went with the gown.

As she put them down on the floor she said:

"These might not fit you, but perhaps you've got something of your own in that bag."

"Yes, I have," Donela answered, "so do not worry about me, but have some sleep."

Even talking about sleep made Kitty start yawning.

"And you do the same," she replied. "I'm quite certain we'll be up 'til dawn, then we've got that horrible journey back to London again."

She went from the room as she finished speaking.

Donela began to undress, hanging her clothes up carefully in the wardrobe.

She thought it must be a very hectic and exhausting

career if they had to perform until dawn.

The Earl of Huntingford must be paying Basil Banks a considerable sum if they were ready to come all the way from London for one performance.

'It will be exciting to see him,' she thought, 'but I am glad to have only one song to sing.'

She wondered, however, what had happened to make Daisy's wig slip.

She supposed dancing could be very strenuous if they put enough energy into it.

She put on one of her nightgowns and slipped between the sheets.

Then because she was really very tired she fell asleep.

* * *

Donela awoke with a start as Kitty came into the room, saying:

"Come on, come on! Basil's clucking like an old hen in case we're late, but as I've told him over and over again, there's plenty of time. At these parties no one hurries themselves!"

Donela sat up.

Kitty had on her wig, and her face was even more made up than it had been when they arrived.

Her eye-lashes were heavily mascaraed until they seemed about an inch long. Her lips were crimson.

She looked very pretty and very theatrical.

With Kitty hurrying her, Donela put on her muslin wrap and sat down on the stool in front of the dressing-table.

With skilful fingers Kitty wound her own hair round her head and pinned it tightly into place.

Then she covered it with a fair wig which was identical to the one she herself was wearing.

It certainly made Donela look strange and not in the least like herself.

In fact, she looked very like Kitty.

"We really might be sisters," she laughed.

Basil Banks put his head round the door.

"His Lordship's 'turned up trumps,'" he said. "There's an excellent meal waiting for us in the Sitting-Room, but you'll have to hurry up."

Kitty gave a cry of delight.

"I'm hungry," she said, "and you know it's a mistake to drink too much on an empty stomach."

She gave a last pat to Donela's wig, saying:

"I'll do your face after we've eaten."

They went into the Sitting-Room, where Daisy joined them.

As Basil Banks had said, the Earl had certainly "turned up trumps."

There was delicious food, most of it cold, and Kitty and Daisy piled their plates high.

Donela was not really hungry, but she thought it would be a mistake not to eat something.

She therefore helped herself to a sliver of cold salmon and afterwards a fruit salad.

"You should eat while you've got the chance," Daisy said. "If you're going off on your own and having to pay for your food, that's the time to 'pull in your belt.'"

"Don't frighten her," Kitty said, "and perhaps

she'll be such a success tonight that she won't have to work for her living."

She spoke, Donela thought, spontaneously.

But surprisingly she saw Basil Banks frown at her.

She thought he was being considerate.

He was telling the girls not to frighten her at the idea of wandering about alone.

He did not allow them to linger over their food but kept glancing at his watch.

Finally he said to Kitty:

"You've eaten enough to fill an elephant! Come on, back to work!"

"You're a slave-driver, that's what you are!" Kitty complained.

Nevertheless she rose from the table and went ahead of Donela back into her bedroom.

Donela sat down on the stool and Kitty mascaraed her eye-lashes.

She also rouged her cheeks and made her lips into a perfect Cupid's bow.

When Donela looked in the mirror she was certain even her mother would not recognise her.

Lastly she put on the gown in which Milly had sung "Won't You Play with Me?"

With a feeling of consternation Donela realised its *décolletage* was very low.

In fact, it was so low that it made her feel embarrassed.

"I cannot wear this!" she exclaimed.

"You've got to!" Kitty replied. "And what does it matter? You're only singing. You haven't got to move about."

"It is too low!" Donela persisted.

The skirt was enormous, a crinoline which had only just gone out of fashion.

It was a "Picture Gown," and it certainly was right for the part.

Made of a stiff taffeta, it was a very pale blue with small bunches of musk-roses on every flounce.

Roses were also grouped where the neckline was off-the-shoulder.

There was an artificial rose on a piece of velvet to go round Donela's long neck.

A rose was sewn onto velvet to make a bracelet for each of her wrists.

"It is very pretty," Donela conceded as Kitty did her up at the back, "but it really is very . . . low in the front and I feel . . . embarrassed."

"Nothing like that bothers Milly!" Kitty said. "Still, I tell you what I'll do—we'll take a rose off the back of the gown and pin it at the front where you think it's low. But don't tell Basil! He don't like us messing about with the dresses."

She cut off a rose as she had said she would.

Donela managed to pull the sides of the gown together and join them with a safety-pin.

The rose certainly made her feel more decent.

Yet she still seemed to be showing an enormous amount of naked shoulder and chest.

'Perhaps they will not notice me,' she thought, 'and as I am singing "A Voice in the Dark," they ought to turn down the lights, if that is possible.'

They went downstairs and crept in at the back of the Dining-Room.

Donela saw that there was no question of altering the lights as if they were in a Theatre.

What had been arranged was a small stage about two feet high at the far end of the Dining-Room.

There were windows looking onto the garden.

At the other end of the room there was a sideboard and a door through which the food was carried.

The stage was not very wide, but long.

It left a small space on either side of it where they could wait and also see without being seen.

There were a number of pot-plants and ferns on either side of the stage.

But there was nothing in front to impede the performers from stepping into the Dining-Room and joining the diners.

There were curtains at the back and at the sides.

The only thing on the stage itself was a piano.

The girls and Basil Banks slipped in through a door.

They found themselves at the side of the stage.

The noise in the Dining-Room seemed suddenly overwhelming.

There was the chatter of voices and loud laughter.

Donela thought there were more people there than she had expected.

As Basil Banks had said, the Earl had invited all those who had taken part in the Point-to-Point.

She had thought there would be perhaps twenty gentlemen present, but not more.

Now, by the noise, she was certain she had underestimated the number.

Then she thought she could hear women's voices.

She parted the leaves of the plants at the side of the stage.

She peeped through them into the Dining-Room.

It was then she saw there were at least forty people round a huge table.

Most of the gentlemen had a woman sitting beside them.

Then, as she looked closer, she saw that the women did not, as she expected, look like her mother.

Their faces were made up, and they looked like Kitty and Daisy.

She remembered then that Basil Banks had said that at some stag-parties the gentlemen brought their lady-friends.

She suddenly knew that this was definitely not the sort of party at which she should be present.

Her mother had explained to her when they had talked about the Music Halls that no lady would go to such a place.

Lady Grayson herself had never thought of visiting one.

"I should not have come here," Donela told herself.

Then she thought it did not matter what the guests were like.

She, Kitty, and Daisy were only entertainers.

Whatever happened in the Dining-Room need not concern them.

Basil Banks was giving Kitty and Daisy instructions about the stage.

They were hardly listening to him.

They knew exactly what to do, and there was no need to be told.

They were wearing long skirts in a brilliant pink which were very frilly and flamboyant.

Their bodices, which were tight-fitting, were also, Donela thought, very low in the front.

Yet they certainly looked very attractive with their wigs and their painted faces.

It would be very disappointing, she thought, if the diners did not appreciate them.

"Now, all three of you come on first and curtsy," Basil Banks was saying, "with Donela in the middle. When she leaves the stage, you do your turn."

He paused a moment and then went on:

"When you have finished, I will sing and after that Donela will do her song, then you come back on again."

Donela was listening intently, but to the other two it was just routine.

"When they finish, Donela," he said, "you come on to the applause, and curtsy as you did at the beginning."

At that moment a servant opened the door behind them to say:

"His Lordship says to begin, Mr. Banks."

"Very good," Basil Banks replied.

He was looking very resplendent, Donela thought, in a stiff white shirt with an enormous diamond stud in the centre of it.

His tail-coat had the same padded shoulders as he had worn in the daytime.

As he swaggered onto the stage he was wearing

his top-hat at an angle on his dark head.

When he appeared there was silence for a moment.

Then, as he said something which Donela did not understand, there was a roar of laughter.

He sat down at the piano and played a few chords.

He told a story which was also greeted with laughter which seemed to shake the chandeliers over the diners' heads.

Donela was not listening to what Basil Banks was saying.

She was peeping through the plants again.

Now she could see the Earl quite clearly.

He was seated at the top of the table in a high-backed chair which she thought was carved with his coat-of-arms.

He was not in the least what she had expected him to be.

She had somehow imagined him, from what they had said, to be lofty and unattractive.

Instead of which she could see, even at a distance, that he was extremely good-looking.

He had clear-cut features and dark hair brushed back from a square forehead.

He was not laughing uproariously like most of his friends.

But he was smiling as if what was happening amused him.

'I am sure the whole evening is going to be a success,' she thought.

Another roar of laughter had greeted what Basil Banks had just said.

Now he went into a song which Donela had never heard before.

Then she realised it had a number of double entendres which she was unable to understand.

It certainly amused the company.

She thought, too, there were references to real people whom they knew, but of whom she had never heard.

As the song finished Kitty said in a whisper:

"Come on, we're next."

She took one of Donela's hands as she spoke, and Daisy took the other.

Then, as everybody was clapping, Basil Banks rose from the piano to take a bow.

He waved his arms for silence and, as they quietened a little, he said:

"And now, Ladies and Gentlemen—my *pièce de résistance*—the sparkling jewels you are waiting to see—my '*Three Belles*'!"

He sat down again at the piano and broke into a romantic but animated Waltz.

There was a pause when Kitty deliberately waited, knowing all eyes would be on the stage.

Then she went forward with Donela and Daisy following her.

When they reached the centre of the stage, all three curtsied together.

The diners, obviously delighted at their appearance, clapped them.

They curtsied twice, then, as Donela moved away, the music changed to an animated and lively dance.

Kitty and Daisy were kicking their legs, showing

frill upon frill of lacy petticoats as they did so.

There were shouts from the audience, but Donela was not watching them.

She had once again parted the leaves to look at the guests.

She could see they were all gentlemen and all the type of friends which her step-father entertained.

The only difference was that they were much younger.

Then, as if irresistibly drawn, her eyes went once again to the Earl.

While everybody else was watching the stage, she thought that now he was looking somewhat bored.

She saw to her surprise that he did not have a woman beside him as most of his guests had.

Instead, on either side of him there was a man.

He started to speak to one of them, who was obviously as little interested in what was going on on the stage as he was.

Donela felt sure that what they were talking about was horses!

chapter four

WHEN Kitty and Daisy finished their dance, there was loud applause.

One or two of the diners shouted "Bravo!"

They came hurrying off the stage, and Kitty said in a whisper to Donela:

"You'll be next after Basil's finished, and don't be nervous."

Donela went to the entrance.

All she could see from there was the stage itself with its colourful plants.

Basil Banks was telling a story which provoked a roar of laughter.

He went into a song which apparently they all knew.

One or two of the gentlemen joined in the Chorus.

When it came to an end he said:

"And now, Ladies and Gentlemen, one of my most beautiful Belles will sing for you, and I feel sure you'll find her irresistible."

He made a sound on the piano like a roll of drums.

Then, as Donela walked on, he started softly to play the music of her song.

For a moment she felt afraid.

Then she told herself nobody knew her and she would never see them again.

What was important was that she should not let down the people who had befriended her.

She therefore forced herself not to think of the crowded Dining-Room.

She was just singing to the girls with whom she had been at School in Florence.

Basil Banks was playing the Chorus, and as he looked towards her she knew when she must begin.

"I'm afraid of your laughter, I'm shy of your
        smile.
I find that I blush after talking awhile,
But I knew when you kissed me last night in
        the Park,
That I love—yes, I do love your voice in the
        the dark."

Donela had no idea that her voice was very different from what the audience was expecting from a girl who habitually sang at Evans's Supper Rooms.

It was very clear and true.

It also had a very young quality about it which made the diners listen in silence.

By the time she had finished, having sung the Verse and the Chorus again, there was hardly a sound in the Dining-Room.

Then, as she sank down in a low curtsy, there was more applause than anyone else had had.

She curtsied again.

Then, as she would have left the stage, there were shouts of "*Encore, encore!*"

"Give them another Chorus!" Basil Banks said in a voice that only she could hear.

Because Donela felt it was slightly banal, she sang the first lines.

Then she moved into a graceful dance that she had learnt in Florence.

It was really meant to be performed with a partner.

But she managed to twirl round so that her full skirt floated out.

As the cheers began, she went into a lower curtsy than she had before.

As she left the stage, Basil Banks said:

"Good! Very good! I'm very proud of you!"

She smiled at him.

He did not allow the applause to die away before he started another of his stories which produced the usual loud guffaws of laughter.

At the side of the stage Donela gave a deep sigh of relief.

It was over!

Then she looked at the two girls who had changed for the next turn.

Or rather, to her horror, they had undressed.

For one second she thought they were naked.

Then she realised they were wearing what appeared to be very long stockings right up to the tops of their legs.

Donela had no idea what the entertainments were like in the Music Halls.

She only knew that the way Kitty and Daisy appeared now was outrageous.

Kitty knew she was staring at them in horror and she said:

"I suppose you've never seen tights before!"

"Is that what . . . you are . . . wearing?" Donela asked.

"They come from America," Kitty explained in a whisper, "and they've got all of London talking about them."

Donela was not surprised.

Now, as she looked closely, she could see that the girls' legs were covered.

But it was with a mesh that was so fine that they might just as well have been naked.

Above them they wore a very tight bodice which ended just below the hips.

It was cut very low so that it showed the little valley between their breasts.

That they looked attractive she could not deny.

Yet how could any decent woman be so brazen?

When, two minutes later, they went onto the stage, there were shrill whistles, shouts, and laughter as well as applause.

As she had no wish to watch what they were doing, Donela went again to her peep-hole.

There was no doubt that now the gentlemen were

enthralled by what was happening on the stage.

The women with them were looking somewhat sour because they had lost their attention.

Irresistibly, Donela's eyes moved towards the Earl.

She thought now that, while he was looking at the stage, there was a cynical twist to his lips.

At the same time, he was too far away for her to be certain it was not her imagination.

Whatever acrobatic feats they were performing, Daisy and Kitty were certainly a success.

When they came off, Basil Banks moved into the centre of the stage and started to play a popular tune on a small guitar.

Donela had not realised that it had been lying on top of the piano.

She thought it was clever of him to play it so well.

What was more, when he repeated the Chorus he did a tap-dance as he was playing.

It was a short turn.

She was not aware until he had finished that Kitty and Daisy had undressed even further.

Now, to her astonishment, they had removed their tight-fitting bodice.

They were wearing only their tights and a garland of flowers around their waists.

Donela was deeply shocked.

She knew her mother would have been appalled and horrified.

How could she appear with two young women who to all intents and purposes were completely naked?

Of course she had never heard of the *poses plastiques* which had come from the Continent.

They had, in fact, been performed in London in a number of low Taverns and Supper Clubs.

Before tights were invented, the girls doing the posing had been actually naked but were not supposed to move.

The curtain had been drawn back to reveal them standing in a provocative or picturesque position.

This they held until the curtain closed again.

Kitty and Daisy, although Donela did not watch them, came onto the stage.

They took up a provocative pose and stood still for a few seconds.

Then they performed another and yet another.

Each one was cheered by the gentlemen in the audience.

There was no doubt the performance was a huge success.

Then, as the girls came rushing off, Basil sang his last song while they put on their clothes again.

"Give us a hand, dearie," Kitty said to Donela.

She was so thankful that they were dressing before joining the party that she was only too willing to do so.

She realised their tight bodices did up down the front.

She therefore picked up their frilly petticoats and wide skirts and helped fasten them at the back.

It was amazing how quickly they managed to dress themselves and look just as they had when the show started.

Less than two minutes later Kitty was walking onto

the stage holding Donela by the hand with Daisy on her other side.

They curtsied.

Then, as the applause began to diminish, Kitty stepped off the stage onto the Dining-Room floor.

Pulling Donela with her, she made straight for the top of the table.

As the three of them reached the Earl, he rose to his feet to shake them by the hand.

"Thank you," he said in a deep voice, "for your really excellent performance which undoubtedly pleased my guests."

"We hope you liked it," Kitty said.

"How could I do anything else?" he replied.

Footman were putting extra chairs into position at the table.

Donela found herself sitting next to the Earl.

Kitty was with the man on his right, and Daisy with the one on his left.

They were the two men she had noticed when she peeped through the plants and who had no women with them.

Servants poured out glasses of champagne, and as Donela lifted hers, the Earl said:

"You are new. I have not seen you before."

Donela was surprised.

"How do you know that?" she asked.

"I am not blind," the Earl replied. "Where is the girl who was performing at Evans's last week?"

"Milly was taken ill," Donela replied, "and so I took her place at the last moment."

"I have not seen you at Evans's!"

She did not answer, and after a moment he asked:
"Why not?"

Donela smiled.

"I have never been to Evans's Supper Rooms."

"That accounts for it," the Earl said, "and I think it was very clever of Banks to find somebody so attractive to take Milly's place."

He turned his chair round to talk to her.

Because she thought he was looking at her penetratingly, it made her feel uncomfortable.

Then she told herself he would never imagine for one moment that she was not what she was pretending to be.

But it would be a mistake for him to ask her too many questions.

"Will you tell me," she said, "if you won the Point-to-Point today?"

"As a matter of fact, I did!" he replied. "How do you know about it?"

"Mr. Banks said the party was for those who had taken part in it. There must have been some excellent horses if the course was difficult."

"It was very difficult," the Earl replied, "so you are quite right. Are you interested in horses?"

"I love riding, if that is what you are asking," Donela replied.

"Then we certainly have a bond in common," the Earl said.

"I am sure your horses are magnificent!" Donela remarked.

"I suppose by that you mean you would like to see them."

"I would love to," Donela said, "but I am afraid as Mr. Banks is leaving very early for London tomorrow, there will be no chance."

She wondered as she spoke whether if she told the Earl she might stay in the village, he would invite her to look at his stables.

Then she knew it would be a reprehensible thing to do.

She would certainly be imposing on her position which was merely that of an entertainer for the evening.

She therefore said nothing.

But she was aware that the Earl was still scrutinising her in a manner she did not understand.

Then he said:

"If your name is not Milly, you must tell me what it is."

"Donela."

"A very unusual name. I do not think I have ever heard it before, and certainly not at any of the Supper Clubs!"

"It is Latin," Donela explained, "and, of course, is a female name derived from Donald."

She was not aware that the Earl looked surprised.

As if he were still thinking of what they had said previously, he asked:

"Do you ride in London?"

"I have not been to London for some time," Donela answered without thinking, "but of course I ride in the country."

The Earl raised his eye-brows. Then he said:

"I imagine the man who mounts you has some excellent horses!"

"They are certainly very well bred," Donela replied, thinking as she spoke of her step-father's stables.

Then, as the Earl did not speak, she said:

"Do you often have Steeple-Chases?"

"Yes," he replied, "and if you are interested, I am riding in the 'Gentlemen's Amateur Race' at Epsom on Thursday, and hoping I shall be the winner."

"I have heard of that race," Donela said, "and I believe they deliberately make it very hard because the riders, who are nearly all owners, are shown how much they expect from their jockeys."

The Earl put back his head and laughed.

"I have never thought of that before," he said, "but of course you are right, and it is a very hard race, which is exactly why I want to win it."

"Tell me about the horse you are going to ride."

"It is the favourite," the Earl replied, "and his name is Rajah."

He smiled before he added:

"Are you going to put your money on me?"

"I will pray for your success, which is far more important," Donela said. "I do not like gambling."

"Why not?"

She realised the Earl had a sharp way of asking questions which made it difficult not to answer him.

She thought for a moment before she said:

"I have read how rich men have lost a fortune through gambling, and how it has ruined their lives—especially in the Regency period."

She paused for a moment before she added:

"Beau Brummell had to go into exile, and politicians like Fox were obsessed by the green baize tables."

"So apart from being a singer and a rider," the Earl said, "you are also a book-lover."

"Of course!" Donela said. "And, I expect, as this is a magnificent house, you have a very big Library."

"I do indeed," the Earl said, "and I am sure you will commend me when I tell you that I add to it every week."

"That is the best thing to do," Donela said. "I always think it sad that so many famous Libraries are not kept up-to-date."

Her mother had told her this.

They had also read about it in several serious articles in *The Times* newspaper.

It said that in great ancestral houses the Libraries, like the Picture Galleries, had stopped being replenished at the beginning of the century.

The Earl was just about to answer when there was a disturbance half-way down the table.

One of his guests had risen to his feet only to collapse on the floor.

Servants had hurried to pick him up.

They carried him from the room followed by the woman who had been sitting next to him.

"Is he ill?" Donela asked innocently. "Are you going to send for a Doctor?"

"He is merely suffering from too much wine," the Earl replied briefly.

Donela looked shocked.

"I never thought of that!" she said. "Surely gentlemen do not get drunk at parties like this?"

"That, I am afraid, is exactly what happens at parties like this!" the Earl replied.

Donela looked down the table.

While she had been talking to the Earl she had been looking at him.

Her mother had taught her that it was rude not to concentrate on the person to whom one was talking.

Now she saw that several of the Earl's guests were crimson in the face.

Two had slipped forward in their chairs so that their heads were resting on the table.

Others—and she could hardly believe it possible—were kissing the women they were sitting next to.

It flashed through her mind that it was like the feasts given by the Romans.

In fact, this was an orgy.

Her eyes travelled down the table again.

Now she saw a man at the end of it pull the woman next to him to her feet.

Then with his arm around her they staggered across the room to the door.

The Earl was watching the expression in her eyes, and after a moment he said:

"I think we would all be wise to move into the Drawing-Room. It will not be so easy to drink so much as it is here."

"I . . . I think that . . . is a good . . . idea," Donela replied.

The Earl beckoned to the Butler, who was standing behind his chair.

He gave him some instructions which Donela could not hear.

She was watching the guests at the table.

She thought how extraordinary it was that because there were no Ladies present, the gentlemen should behave in such an outrageous manner.

If her mother or any of her friends had been the hostess, everybody would have behaved with the utmost propriety.

The Earl rose to his feet.

"Come along," he said to Donela, "if we lead the way, the others will follow. I have sent a message to Banks to play in the Drawing-Room."

He had been playing all the time they were talking.

Donela thought it rather sad that no one appeared to be paying him any attention.

"I think he plays very well," she said now.

"So do I," the Earl agreed, "and I would like to hear you sing again, but not tonight."

Donela suspected that he was thinking he could hear her at Evans's Supper Rooms.

If that was what he intended, she thought, he would be disappointed.

She wondered if perhaps he would be looking for her as her step-father might be doing.

It was rather a joke to think she could come in and out of people's lives, only to vanish like a *geni* out of a bottle.

She walked beside the Earl to the Drawing-Room.

Kitty and the man to whom she had been talking was just behind them.

Realising what was happening, the other guests

began one by one to get to their feet, some very unsteadily.

The Butler opened the door.

They went into a room which Donela had not seen before.

She thought it was one of the most attractive she had ever seen.

There were three huge crystal chandeliers hanging from the ceiling on which the candles were all alight.

The furniture was French and she thought the pictures were too.

There was a grand piano in an alcove.

A few seconds later she heard Basil Banks start to play one of Offenbach's lilting tunes.

He was playing more serious music than she had heard him play before.

She was aware that he was, in fact, a very accomplished pianist.

She wondered why he was not a professional musician rather than a "Supper Room Entertainer."

"You are very serious!" the Earl remarked. "And that I cannot allow!"

"Why not?" Donela asked.

"Because this is supposed to be a night of gaiety."

There was something mocking in the way he spoke.

She was sure he despised the behaviour of some of his guests.

There was now an undoubtedly cynical twist to his lips.

She thought she had seen it when she had peeped at him from the side of the stage.

She sat down on a sofa.

As his guests came into the Drawing-Room, the Earl pointed out the card-tables.

A number had been erected at one end of the room.

In the centre the carpet had been removed so that there was a dance-floor just in front of the piano.

A man and a woman, clinging very closely to each other, started to dance.

Several other couples joined them.

Donela saw Daisy taking the man whom she had been next to in the Dining-Room onto the floor.

As he pulled her close to him, she put her arms round his neck.

It was then Donela was afraid she would be expected to behave in the same way.

She looked round for the Earl.

He was at the end of the room, arranging players at one of the card-tables.

Quickly she got to her feet.

Moving towards a door near to the fireplace, she slipped out of the Drawing-Room.

She found herself in an Ante-Room which was beautifully furnished and also lit by a chandelier.

There was no one there.

As she expected, she saw another door which she was sure would open onto the corridor.

She was not mistaken.

There were still guests staggering along it from the Drawing-Room.

They did not notice her as she slipped away in the other direction.

She went up the stairs which she had climbed when she first arrived.

As she turned towards her bedroom, she thought with relief that she had escaped.

She could not imagine anything to be more degrading than for her to dance in the same way as Daisy.

It also horrified her to think that she might be partnered by one of the gentlemen who had had too much to drink.

She had almost reached her bedroom when a housemaid came hurrying toward her.

"Be you Miss Donela?" she asked.

"Yes, I am," Donela replied, rather surprised that the maid should know her name.

"Yer room's been moved," the housemaid said. "I've already taken along yer belongings."

"Moved?" Donela enquired. "Why?"

" 'is Lordship's orders. 'E thinks ye'd be more comfortable."

Donela was surprised.

She had thought the room into which she had been shown when she arrived was quite a pleasant one.

There was nothing particularly unusual about it.

It was certainly better than anything she might have found in the Village Inn.

"If ye'll come this way," the housemaid was saying, "I'll show ye where ye're to sleep."

She walked ahead.

Donela was acutely aware that she disapproved of her in the same way the Housekeeper had when they arrived.

"This is what comes of being an actress!" she told herself with a smile.

It was something she would like to have laughed about with her mother.

Then she remembered that her mother would be horrified if she knew what was happening to her at the moment.

She would certainly have been appalled if she had witnessed the drunkenness of the Earl's guests.

'I suppose when I go home it is something I will not be able to tell anyone,' Donela thought.

The housemaid was flouncing ahead at what seemed an unnecessary speed.

They had now reached the centre of the great building.

They passed the main staircase which was very impressive.

The corridor on the other side of it was furnished with some very beautiful French Commodes.

Donela was looking at one of them when the housemaid stopped and opened a door.

"'Ere's where ye are," she said in a cold voice. "I've brought along yer belongings but not the—trunk."

She spoke as if that was too dirty for her to touch.

"Thank you very much," Donela said. "I would be grateful if you would help me out of the gown I am wearing."

She walked to the dressing-table as she spoke.

As the maid started to undo the buttons of her huge-skirted "Picture Gown," she took off her wig.

She placed it on the dressing-table before she said:

"As we will be leaving early in the morning, I wonder if you would be kind enough to put this wig in the box in which it belongs. You will find it on the dressing-table of the room I have just left."

"I sees it there," the housemaid replied.

"Put the wig into the box very carefully, and the gown is to be packed on top of the trunk."

She thought as she spoke that it would be very unkind if the wig or the gown should be damaged in any way.

Milly, when she was better, would be upset if they were both in a mess.

As she spoke she stepped out of the gown and also the stiff petticoat that went underneath it.

The maid put them both over her arm.

When she would have picked up the wig, Donela gave her the rose on velvet ribbons which had been round her neck and on her wrists.

"I am sure you will pack these very carefully," she said. "And where is my hand-bag?"

"In th' drawer," the maid answered.

Donela opened it and took half-a-sovereign from her purse.

"This is for you," she said, "and thank you for looking after me."

The maid's hands were full.

But there was a small pocket in her white apron, and Donela put the half-a-sovereign into it.

She thought the maid looked surprised as she did so, then she said:

"Thank ye! I'll see these 'ere things be well packed."

"I know you will," Donela said, "and I am very grateful."

Because the maid's hands were full, Donela ran to open the door for her.

As she went past her, she said:

"I hopes ye enjoy yerself."

Then she was hurrying down the corridor.

As Donela shut the door, she thought it was a strange thing for her to say.

She would have gone on undressing but stopped to turn the key in the lock.

She remembered what Daisy had said about "human ghosts" knocking on the door if she had stayed at the Inn.

With so many gentlemen in the house who had had a lot to drink, it would be easy for one of them to mistake her room for his.

When she and her mother had travelled to Worcestershire from Portsmouth, they had stayed at Posting Inns on the way.

They had shared a room, not only because it was cheaper, but also because her mother did not want her to sleep alone.

Mrs. Colwyn, as she had been then, had always locked the door.

"Why do you do that, Mama?" Donela enquired.

"We do not want people bursting in on us," her mother said. "Besides, you must always remember there are thieves about who might try to steal our possessions."

"And when there are not any thieves?" Donela asked.

"It is always better to be safe than sorry," her mother replied.

Donela sat down in front of the mirror to take the pins from her hair.

As she did so she thought that with the door locked, she would be safe.

She doubted anyway that it was likely there were thieves in the Earl's house.

Like her step-father's, the staff would be scrupulously honest.

If they were dismissed without a reference, they would never obtain another position in a gentleman's establishment.

Her hair had been crushed by the wig and wanted brushing.

She gave it at least the hundred strokes which her Nanny had always told her was the right thing to do.

Then she washed, removing all the cosmetics from her face before she put on her nightgown.

After opening the window behind the curtains she got into bed.

Because she had slept so badly the night before, she was really very tired.

The huge canopied and curtained bed was not only impressive but exceedingly comfortable.

"It was very kind of the Earl to move me to this grand room!" she told herself.

She was a little afraid that if they knew about it, Kitty and Daisy might be jealous.

'I suppose I was just lucky because the Earl had no lady beside him,' she thought.

Then she blew out the candles on her bedside-tables and closed her eyes.

It was very quiet and she felt herself drifting away.

*   *   *

Donela was dreaming that she was riding a magnificent black stallion and approaching nearer and nearer to a very high jump.

She was just about to put the stallion over it when she was aware of a voice.

For a moment it seemed a part of her dream.

Then she heard a man say:

"Are you really asleep, or just pretending?"

He seemed somehow muddled up with the horse which she was riding.

Then as she opened her eyes she was aware there was a light beside her and a man was sitting on the side of the bed, looking at her.

For a moment she could not believe it was happening.

Then she saw to her astonishment that it was the Earl.

chapter five

THE Earl had walked back from the card-tables to the sofa where he had left Donela.

To his surprise she was not there.

He looked round and realised she was not on the dance-floor, nor was she anywhere else in the Drawing-Room.

He then thought she must have gone upstairs to bed.

It amused him because, when he was with a woman, she never left him if there was a chance of their being together.

Because he was so handsome, so rich, and so important, he had been pursued by women from the moment he left Eton.

He would have been inhuman if he had not enjoyed

their favours and that they flattered, complimented, and fawned on him.

At the same time, as he grew older, he very quickly became bored with whoever was his favourite at the moment.

He had one *affaire de coeur* after another, but the fires which flared so brilliantly at the beginning died quicker year by year.

Then he would bring the liaison to a close.

If there was one thing he disliked, it was continuing with what was lukewarm and not the ecstatic enjoyment it had been at the start.

He was, in fact, very fastidious.

He was easily put off if a woman, however beautiful, had what he called "irritating tricks."

He had discarded one of the most beautiful women in England simply because she twirled her rings while he talked to her.

Another affair with a delightful and exotic Frenchwoman came to an abrupt end.

She was continually touching him with her long, elegant fingers, even in public.

When he was in London he did nothing to add to his reputation as a *Roué*.

Of course people gossiped.

He was far too handsome and attractive for them not to want to talk about him on every possible occasion.

He was, however, very protective of his family name and also his position in Society.

He would never have thought of giving a riotous

party such as was taking place tonight, at his house in Park Lane.

There, he entertained Statesmen, politicians, the leading figures of the Social World, and quite a number of Royalty.

There was no need for him to have, as so many of his contemporaries had, an attractive Ballerina, or an actress from Drury Lane in a discreet little house in St. John's Wood.

He had only to look with interest at any of the beautiful women who graced the Balls at Devonshire House.

They would move towards him as if mesmerised.

He had come to the country for the Point-to-Point.

It took place every year on his estate and he intended to give a "Stag Party."

He liked the company of his fellow men.

He enjoyed it more than anything else when they could talk about their horses.

It was a subject in which he was particularly interested.

Nobody knew more about the breeding and performance of the horses taking part in the "Sport of Kings."

The party was arranged.

Then two of his friends asked if they could bring the women in whom they were interested with them.

Both of the girls in question were performing in the *corps de ballet* at Covent Garden.

The Earl thought it would be a mistake to have only two women present.

He therefore asked the rest of his guests if they wished to bring someone with them.

To his surprise, every man accepted with the exception of two neighbours.

As they lived some distance away, they asked if they could stay the night.

But they told him they would be alone.

At the last moment the Earl remembered that the three girls who were Basil Banks's *Belles* were extremely attractive.

He often dined at Evans's Supper Rooms.

Strangely, he enjoyed the unusual entertainment provided by the Proprietor.

It was, in fact, the best in London.

The vocalists were particularly well-chosen, the French and Italian singers unique.

It was on an impulse that he thought those for whom he was giving the house-party would enjoy "*Basil Banks and His Belles*."

Because he was of such importance, the Proprietor of the Supper Rooms agreed to replace them with another Act.

The Earl, of course, paid for the privilege.

It cost him quite a considerable sum to persuade Banks to take his girls to the country, then back again to London the next day.

Once the Earl had set his sights on something he wanted, it was very difficult for anyone to refuse him.

As he sat at the top of the table, he was aware of the enthusiasm with which his friends applauded the Show.

He told himself somewhat ruefully that it would

be something which would have to be repeated every year.

The *poses plastiques* came to an end.

It was obvious that the two men on either side of him were eager to meet the *Belles*.

Inevitably, this left him with the third *Belle*, who was wearing the "Picture Gown."

The Earl had, in fact, been astonished when Donela sang.

He had heard Milly sing "Who Will Play with Me?" which was a very suggestive song.

She had put it over extremely well.

But it was certainly not a song he would have allowed in his Drawing-Room in Park Lane.

Donela's clear, child-like voice had a purity which was striking. After she had sung the first lines, she was listened to in silence.

The Earl knew that this was unusual for the company of people who were sitting round his table.

On these occasions they listened to nothing but the sound of their own voices.

He also was aware that the men were more interested in the looks of Kitty and Daisy, especially their high kicks, than anything they could sing or say.

By the time Donela made her final curtsy, he was not only aware that she was not Milly.

He was intrigued as to how Banks had discovered anyone so different from the usual performers at Evans's.

When Donela had sat down next to him at the table, he could see how pretty she was.

She spoke in an educated voice which was very unlike that of the other two *Belles*.

He knew when they went into the Drawing-Room that he wanted to know more about her.

He sorted out his other guests.

He made sure that those who were more sober than the rest had tables at which they could play Whist.

Then he went in search of Donela.

He had a suspicion that she had gone away because she thought the rest of the party was behaving badly.

At the same time, she was convinced he would follow her.

He had told the Butler to have her room moved to another which was near to his own.

He had no intention of visiting the part of the house where the other entertainers were sleeping.

It was some time before he was able to go upstairs.

The party was dwindling rapidly as couple after couple disappeared together.

Finally only the Whist-players were left.

The women beside them were yawning, obviously bored by their concentration on cards.

The Earl brought the evening to a close.

He saw somewhat pointedly that he suspected they were all tired after such an arduous day.

As he went upstairs the servants started to extinguish the candles in the sconces.

When the Earl reached his own room his Valet was waiting for him and he undressed quickly.

He thought it had been a good party with the exception of a few men who had drunk too much.

He blamed himself for allowing the wine to flow too freely.

He knew that a number of the riders had been eating and drinking very little for the last two weeks.

They wanted to get their weight down for the race.

Now that it was over, they had drunk a large amount of champagne before dinner.

This, combined with a very fine vintage wine in the Dining-Room, had proved too much.

Because he was very abstemious himself, the Earl could not understand a man who did not know how to hold his liquor.

The excuse was that those who had offended had been very young.

He was certain they would be suitably apologetic tomorrow.

When his Valet left him, he was wearing a long velvet robe.

He brushed the sides of his hair into place.

Then, crossing the room, he opened the door into the *Boudoir*.

It was a very attractive room which lay between the Master Bedroom and the "Countess's Room."

The *Boudoir* had been decorated by his mother and contained pieces of furniture that she particularly liked.

The paintings were also those she had chosen herself from the Picture Gallery.

Even though she had been dead for five years, the gardeners always gave the Housekeeper flowers to put in her room.

The fragrance of them pleased the Earl as he walked through it.

He reached the door which communicated with the bedroom.

He turned the handle, thinking with a smile that Donela would be waiting for him.

She was undoubtedly wondering why he had taken so long.

To his surprise, the room was in darkness.

He stood for a moment, wondering if she had blown out the lights because she was piqued.

On the other hand, it might be a new approach he had not encountered before.

Usually when he visited a woman in her bedroom, he found her draped elegantly against the lace-edged pillows.

She would have a book in her hand.

If it was the first time he had come to her, she would look up in surprise.

She would exclaim it had never crossed her mind that he would do such a thing!

The Earl turned from the door, and, going back into the Boudoir, picked up a candelabrum containing three candles.

It stood on a table near the fireplace.

Carrying it in his hand, he entered the "Countess's Room."

He could see that Donela was in bed and apparently asleep.

He was sure it was a pretence.

As he drew nearer to the bed, he saw that she

looked very different from how she had in the Drawing-Room.

To begin with, he had never seen anything quite so lovely as her hair.

The light from the candelabrum brought out the flashes of red amongst the gold.

It fell over her shoulders, and he was sure she had arranged it in such an attractive manner before pretending to be asleep.

He put down the candelabrum on the bedside table, then looked down at Donela.

If she was only pretending to be asleep, she was certainly a very good actress.

One of her hands lay outside on the sheet and was relaxed.

Her eye-lashes, which now owed nothing to mascara, were dark against her cheeks.

Her skin, without the paint and powder she had used on the stage, was as translucent as a pearl.

She also looked very young and pretty—no, that was the wrong word—she was lovely.

Lovelier, the Earl thought, than anybody he had seen for a long time.

She appeared to be breathing regularly.

Yet he still thought he was being hoodwinked by somebody who was a great deal cleverer than her predecessors.

He sat down on the side of the bed, and as she still did not stir, he asked:

"Are you asleep, or only pretending?"

It was then that Donela opened her eyes.

He saw that for the moment they were hazy with sleep.

She looked at him and gave a distinct start before she said:

"What . . . has . . . happened . . . what is . . . wrong?"

"There is nothing wrong," the Earl replied, "except that one of my guests went to bed without saying goodnight."

It took Donela a second to understand what he was saying.

Then she replied:

"I . . . I thought it was . . . best. But . . . why are you . . . here?"

"I should have thought that was obvious," the Earl replied.

"But . . . but you should not . . . have come to my room!" Donela said. "And . . . I locked . . . the door!"

"I came in through another door," the Earl explained.

Donela pushed herself up a little higher against the pillows, at the same time pulling the sheet over her breasts.

"It . . . it was kind of you to . . . let me sleep in this . . . beautiful room," she said, "but now . . . you should go."

"Why should I do that?" the Earl asked.

"Because it is . . . wrong for you to be here . . . very wrong!"

The Earl smiled.

"That is a subject on which we disagree, and I

108

think, Donela, as you are very lovely, you must allow me to tell you so, and, of course, kiss you goodnight.''

Donela gave a little cry of horror.

"No . . . no! Of course . . . you cannot . . . do that! Please . . . go away . . . at . . . once!''

The Earl looked at her in surprise.

It certainly sounded as if that was what she wanted.

But he could not believe that anyone who performed with Basil Banks would not have been expecting this to happen.

"I think,'' he said in a voice which most women found irresistible, "that you are angry with me for leaving you alone downstairs, but it was something that could not be avoided, and now you must forgive me.''

He moved a little nearer to her as he spoke.

Donela shrank from him and, holding the sheet even tighter around her, said:

"I . . . I do not . . . know what . . . you are . . . s-saying . . . please . . . please . . . go away . . . and let . . . me sleep.''

"I cannot believe you are saying this,'' the Earl replied. "I promise, Donela, that I will make you happy, and, of course, I will be very grateful.''

He smiled before he said:

"You must tell me which jewel is your favourite. I am sure we can find a necklace which will make you look even lovelier than you did tonight.''

Donela stared at him.

Then, as if vaguely she understood what he was saying, the colour came into her cheeks.

"I do not . . . want . . . anything from . . . you,''

she said, "except that . . . you should . . . leave me . . . alone."

"Think how disappointing that will be for me," the Earl said.

His voice deepened as he said:

"Stop playing games and let us enjoy ourselves!"

He put his hand on her shoulder, and his lips would have found hers if Donela had not screamed:

"Leave . . . me . . . alone! Please . . . leave me . . . alone!"

She put out her hands to push him away from her with all her strength.

She took the Earl by surprise.

As he was sitting on the side of the bed, he was obliged to steady himself.

As he did so, Donela slipped out of bed on the other side.

She ran across the room to the window.

She pulled aside the curtains as if looking for a way of escape.

Then she could see in the moonlight that there was a sharp drop from the window onto the gardens below.

She turned round, her eyes seeming to fill her whole face.

The Earl could see the curves of her figure beneath her nightgown.

It struck him that she was immature, a child rather than a woman.

For a moment he just sat looking at her.

Then he said in a different tone:

"Now, what is all this about?"

"I . . . I am . . . frightened . . . I am . . . trying

to . . . run away!" Donela said with a little cob in her voice.

"There is no need for such dramatics," the Earl replied.

"There is . . . and you . . . have no . . . right to . . . come here . . . and try to . . . kiss me!"

It struck him, although it seemed incredible, that she really did not understand that what he intended did not include only kissing.

For a moment there was silence.

Then he said:

"If I have upset you, I must apologise. Suppose you get back into bed and tell me why you are with Banks and masquerading as one of his *Belles*?"

Donela continued to clutch one of the curtains.

"If . . . if I . . . do that," she said, "will you . . . promise . . . not to . . . touch me?"

"I promise," the Earl agreed, "but we can hardly have a conversation as we are at the moment."

Slowly, like a small animal afraid of being captured, Donela walked back towards the bed.

She got into it on the side from which she had left it, and sat as far from the Earl as possible.

She pulled the sheet up nearly to her neck.

He waited, and when she looked at him, he could see the fear in her eyes.

"Now, suppose we start from the beginning," he said, "and you tell me why you came to my house tonight with people who are notorious for their erotic entertainment in the Supper Rooms of London?"

"I . . . I did not . . . know . . . that," Donela said.

"But you must have known it," the Earl insisted.

"Otherwise you would not have been with them."

There was silence until, almost as if the words were dragged from her, Donela said:

"I . . . I met Mr. Banks . . . in the Stage-Coach."

The Earl stared at her in disbelief.

"In the Stage-Coach?" he exclaimed. "Do you mean you met Basil Banks and his girls for the first time as they were coming here?"

Donela nodded.

"Then why did you come here tonight?"

Donela hesitated.

She thought it was a mistake for the Earl to know too much.

At the same time, as she would be leaving tomorrow, there was no reason why it should be a danger to her personally.

"I am waiting!" the Earl prompted.

"I was . . . in the . . . Stage-Coach," Donela said, "and they told me . . . they were . . . coming here to . . . perform . . . and because I had . . . nowhere to stay . . . the night, they . . . suggested I should . . . join them."

"What do you mean—you had nowhere to stay the night? Where were you going?"

"A-away."

"Away—where—and where from?"

"That is . . . my . . . business."

"I think it has now become mine," the Earl argued. "You came here purporting to be an entertainer from Evans's Supper Rooms, but you are clearly something quite different."

Donela did not answer, and he said:

"I suppose I should have known when I heard you sing and when I talked to you that you were not what you pretended to be, but I was deceived by your wig and the company you were with."

There was a note of rebuke in his voice which made Donela blush, and she said:

"I had no . . . idea that . . . Kitty and Daisy would . . . wear nothing but . . . what they . . . call 'tights' . . . but by . . . then it was . . . too late!"

"Much too late!" the Earl agreed. "And I suppose you did not understand why I had moved you to this room?"

Donela's eyes opened very wide.

"The housemaid said . . . you wanted . . . me to be . . . more comfortable and . . . I thought it was . . . very kind of . . . you."

"And you did not expect me to join you?"

"No . . . of course . . . not!" Donela replied. "How could I have imagined that . . . any gentleman could . . . do such a . . . thing? I think it was . . . wrong and . . . wicked of you!"

"That is what I would expect you to think," the Earl said, "but you must realise that if you take up with strange people in Stage-Coaches, and have no idea where you are going to stay the night, this is the sort of danger in which you will find yourself."

Donela drew in her breath.

"I . . . suppose it was . . . very . . . stupid of me," she agreed, "but I never . . . never thought of . . . anything like that . . . when I . . . ran away."

"So, you have run away!" the Earl exclaimed. "Why?"

Donela realised she had made a mistake and could not look at him.

"I . . . cannot tell you."

"You mean you *will* not tell me."

"It would . . . be a mistake . . . and I have . . . to hide . . . I have to! But I . . . will not let . . . anything like this . . . happen again."

"How can you be sure of that?" the Earl asked.

There was silence until he said:

"Do not be so ridiculous! You cannot go wandering about alone looking so lovely that every man who sees you will want to possess you!"

"I am . . . going to . . . find a . . . quiet village where . . . no one will be the . . . least interested . . . in me," Donela said.

"Even in villages there are men," the Earl remarked.

He saw her give a little shiver.

Then he thought what he was hearing could not be true.

It was surely some new enticement he had not heard of before.

Sharply, so that his voice startled Donela, he said:

"Whose horses were you riding when you were in the country?"

Because it was not what she had expected him to say, Donela told the truth:

"My . . . step-father's."

The Earl looked at her penetratingly.

"If you are lying," he said, "I am sure I would be aware of it."

"I am . . . not lying!" Donela said. "But I do . . . not want to . . . talk about it."

Because she was certain that was what he would go on doing, she said piteously:

"I am tired . . . and you are . . . bullying me! Please . . . please . . . let me go to . . . sleep!"

The Earl hesitated. Then he said:

"Very well, we will talk about it tomorrow. In the meantime, Donela, believe that I am trying to help you."

He rose to his feet and stood looking at her lying on the far side of the bed.

"I have a lot of things to say to you," he said, "but we will leave them until the morning."

She did not move, but he was aware that she was watching him warily.

It was as if she half-suspected he was trying to trick her.

Then, as he picked up the candelabrum and walked towards the communicating door, she said in a very small voice:

"Thank . . . you."

The Earl turned back to look at her.

He thought no one could look more alluring or, in fact, more lovely.

He wondered if he was being deceived.

It seemed incredible she could be as innocent as she appeared to be.

Yet, he felt it was innocence that surrounded her like an aura.

"Goodnight, Donela," he said.

He went from the *Boudoir* and closed the door behind him.

He put down the candelabrum and walked on to his own room.

He could hardly believe it had actually happened.

As he got into bed he went over everything word for word.

He was still not absolutely sure that he had not been a fool.

* * *

When Donela was quite certain he had gone, she lit the candle beside her bed and walked to the communicating door.

As she hoped, there was a key in the lock, and she turned it.

Then she went to the window and looked out.

The moonlight turned the garden into a place of enchantment.

"I must leave," she told herself, "and . . . quickly!"

She went to the wardrobe.

She found, as she expected, that the housemaid had hung up the gown and jacket in which she had arrived.

Her carpet-bag was lying beneath it on the floor of the wardrobe.

It did not take her long to dress.

She packed everything she owned into the carpet-bag.

She had a quick look round the room to make sure she had forgotten nothing.

Very slowly, so as not to make the slightest noise, she turned the key in the lock.

She listened before she opened the door more than a crack.

Everything was very quiet, and she went out into the corridor.

Although the servants had extinguished every other sconce, there was always one candle left burning.

The corridor was full of shadows. At the same time, she could see her way.

She moved noiselessly over the thick carpet, and when she reached the staircase she waited.

She peeped down into the hall.

The night-footman was in his canopied chair and would therefore not see her.

She went on along the passage which led from her first bedroom.

She thought perhaps she ought to tell Basil Banks she was leaving.

Then she decided it would involve explanations.

She could never tell him or anybody else that the Earl had come to her room and tried to kiss her.

She knew how horrified her mother would be.

Besides, Basil Banks might take it upon himself to rebuke the Earl for doing anything so outrageous.

That would also be a mistake.

Once she had disappeared, no-one would worry about her again, least of all the Earl.

She found the secondary staircase up which they had been brought by the footman on their arrival.

Going down it, she moved along the corridor in the direction of the Dining-Room.

She was trying to find a door which would lead out into the garden.

She was sure there would be one.

There were several in her step-father's house which were well bolted at night.

At the same time, it was unlikely anyone would hear her letting herself out.

There was a passage to the left which was in darkness.

She fancied that the door she was seeking would be at the end of it.

She moved along it, finding her way by instinct rather than by what she could see.

Then, unexpectedly, she heard voices.

She stopped, afraid of who she might encounter.

At the same time, she thought it was strange that there should be anyone about at this hour of the night.

It was then she heard a man's voice say:

"Have you done what I told you?"

She could tell from the way he spoke that he was a gentleman.

"It wasn't no use, Guv, he weren't there."

The man who answered his question was obviously uneducated, and she thought he had a Cockney accent.

"What do you mean—not there?" the gentleman enquired.

"Oi goes into 'is room like yer tol' me to," the other man replied, "but th' bird 'ad flown!"

"Damnation!" the gentleman ejaculated. "He

must have been with that bitch who sang to us. It never struck me that he would fancy her!''

''Well, 'e weren't in 'is room, an' that's fer sure!'' the other man said.

''You could have waited,'' the gentleman argued.

''Too dangerous, Guv, an' when a man's wiv a woman wot 'e fancies, 'e don't 'urry 'isself.''

''Curse it!'' the gentleman stormed. ''Then we will have to do it in London. He will be going back to-morrow, or early the next day.''

''Th' race be on Thursday,'' the Cockney said.

''I am aware of that,'' the gentleman replied, ''and if you do not make it impossible for him to ride, I will be bankrupt—do you understand? Only you can save me, and you have to succeed somehow.''

''Oi'll do me best, Guv, but t'aint easy.''

''You will have to get into his house in Park Lane. I will give you a map so that there will not be any more difficulty than finding your way to his room tonight.''

''All Oi 'opes is 'e's in when Oi gets t'ere!'' the Cockney said.

''I told you, you should have waited until he re-turned,'' the gentleman said.

There was silence until he added angrily:

''Go back to London! Here is some money for your fare, and I will see you tomorrow night. This is our last chance—get that into your head!''

''Oi told yer, Guv'nor, Oi done me best!'' the Cockney whined.

There was the sound of a door opening.

It was then that Donela realised not only what she

had heard, but that she herself might be discovered.

With the swiftness of a frightened fawn she turned round and hurried back the way she had come.

She went up the staircase and along the corridor.

Only when she reached her bedroom did she think with horror of what the men had been saying.

The gentleman, whoever he was, intended with his confederate to maim the Earl so that he would be unable to ride in the race on Thursday.

It was a crime she could hardly contemplate.

Yet she remembered the Earl had said his horse was the favourite!

If he withdrew at the last moment, whoever was betting on the next best horse would be able to get a very good price.

Her step-father had explained to her exactly how betting went.

She could understand that the odds on the Earl, who was obviously a very accomplished jockey, would be very short.

"I shall *have* to tell him," she told herself.

Then she thought it was none of her business and the best thing she could do would be to go on her way as she had intended.

By now the other gentleman, whoever he was, would have gone back to bed, while the villain would doubtless be waiting to catch the first Stage-Coach back to London.

It was then Donela knew that she was too frightened to go into the moonlight alone.

Also, it would be both cowardly and dishonest of

her not to tell the Earl what she had overheard.

"Papa would consider it my duty," she told herself.

At the same time, she longed to get away.

She wanted to forget that she had seen Kitty and Daisy in tights.

Also, she was running away from the Earl.

It was humiliating that he had tried to kiss her.

Also, he had offered her a present of jewellery which he thought she would accept because she was an actress.

Donela did not understand exactly what he wanted.

The girls at School had said that actresses accepted gifts of jewellery from gentlemen and often money.

A Lady could accept nothing more valuable than a fan.

"My brother gave a woman he fancied a pair of ruby earrings for Christmas!" a French girl had told Donela. "And all he gave me was a note-book with my initials on it!"

"Was she pretty?" one of the other girls asked.

"How should I know?" the French girl replied. "*Maman* said when I told her that I was not to speak of such 'creatures' and my brother told me to keep my mouth shut."

They had all laughed at this.

Donela thought now that the Earl did not think of her as a Lady.

Although she had driven him away tonight, he might try to kiss her again tomorrow.

At the same time, how could she let him be so badly injured that he could not ride?

With a sigh which seemed to come from the very depths of her body, she started to undress.

chapter six

DONELA awoke as a housemaid came into the room.

She pulled back the curtains and with an effort Donela came back to reality.

"What is the time?" she asked.

"It's half-past ten, Miss," the housemaid replied, "and His Lordship would like to see you when you come downstairs."

Donela sat up abruptly.

"Half-past ten?" she asked. "It cannot be!"

"You were fast asleep, Miss," the housemaid answered, "so I didn't disturb you."

Donela tried to remember what had happened.

As the housemaid brought in her breakfast and set it down beside the bed, she enquired:

"Has Mr. Banks and the two young ladies with him left?"

"Oh, yes, Miss!" the housemaid replied. "They went very early. Half-past eight, I thinks it was."

Donela remembered that the Stage-Coach to London stopped at the gates at nine o'clock.

She had not intended to go with them.

At the same time, she thought it was rude not to have said goodbye.

There was, however, nothing she could do about it, and she started to eat her breakfast.

The housemaid was tidying the room.

Donela realised she was not the same girl who had looked after her last night.

She was an older woman who did not seem so disapproving as the other servant had been.

When Donela had finished her breakfast she brought her some hot water with which to wash.

"I would be grateful if you could pack everything in the carpet-bag I have with me," Donela said, "except for the clothes I will be wearing."

"You're travelling very light, Miss," the housemaid observed.

Donela made no reply.

She was wondering if she could ask the Earl to convey her to the village so that she could take a Stage-Coach to somewhere else.

If he refused, she would have to walk and she knew it was a long distance.

It was a hot day and she would have to carry her jacket as well as her bag.

"It is no use complaining," she chided her reflection in the mirror. "I have to find somewhere to go, or else return home and marry Lord Waltingham!"

She felt herself shiver at the thought.

Resolutely she did her hair neatly and put on the hat which matched her gown.

The housemaid did it up for her and she was ready to go downstairs.

Her brush and comb were put on top of the carpet-bag and once again she tipped the housemaid for looking after her.

She thought rather ruefully this meant she had altogether spent a pound of her precious money.

At the same time, it might have cost her more to stay the night at an Inn.

Donela looked at herself in the mirror before she went down the stairs.

The house seemed very quiet after the noise and chatter of last night.

As she reached the hall the Butler said:

"His Lordship's waiting for you, Miss, in his Study."

As he spoke, he took her bag from her and propped it against one of the chairs in the hall.

Then he went ahead down the corridor.

He opened the door of the Study and Donela saw it was very like her step-father's.

There were portraits of horses on the walls and comfortable furniture covered in leather.

However, she really had eyes only for the Earl, who was sitting at his desk.

He rose as she walked towards him.

He was aware there was a flicker of fear in her eyes, although not the terror he had seen last night.

"Good-morning, Donela!" he said in his deep voice. "I hope you slept well?"

"I am ... ashamed of being ... so late," Donela replied. "But ... before I leave I have ... something to ... tell you."

"Before you leave?" the Earl asked. "Is that what you are determined to do?"

She nodded, and he said:

"I expect you know that Banks and the two girls have already gone back to London?"

"I was not going with them," Donela replied.

"Then where are you going?"

She thought it was a mistake to talk about herself, and she therefore replied:

"I should have gone by now, but I stayed because I have something to tell you."

The Earl walked from behind his desk.

"Suppose we sit down," he said, "and I am, of course, interested in what you have to say."

Donela seated herself on the leather sofa which was on one side of the fireplace.

There was no fire in the grate and the sunshine coming through the window was warm.

She was facing it.

She had no idea that the Earl thought, as the sunshine illuminated her, that she was so lovely, it was almost as if she were a part of it.

He did not speak, and after a short silence Donela began:

"Last night, after you ... after you left me ... I got up and ... dressed."

"Why did you do that?" the Earl asked.

"I . . . I thought it best to . . . go away."

"I cannot imagine why you should do anything so foolish!" he said sharply. "But—you are still here!"

"That is . . . what I am . . . trying to . . . tell you."

"I apologise if I interrupted," he said, "please, continue."

Stammering because he made her nervous, Donela explained.

She had gone down the secondary staircase, trying to find a door into the garden.

Then she had heard voices and knew that two men were talking together in whispers.

"Two men?" the Earl repeated. "What were they doing there at that time of night?"

"One of them was a gentleman," Donela said, "and the other, I am sure, was a Cockney from London."

The Earl stared at her.

"What were they saying?"

"They were . . . planning to . . . injure you," Donela answered, "so that you would not be able to . . . ride in the . . . race on . . . Thursday!"

The Earl was incredulous.

He rose from the chair in which he had been sitting and sat down next to her on the sofa.

"Do not be frightened," he said quietly, "but tell me exactly what you heard them saying."

Donela looked away from him.

Then slowly, trying to remember every word, she repeated what the two men had said to each other.

It took her a little time, and she stumbled once or twice, afraid that she might make a mistake.

She had actually a very retentive memory, as her teachers had told her in Florence.

Once she had learnt a poem or a piece of prose she never forgot a word of it.

She went on as far as the point where she knew the two men would be leaving each other.

"I thought they would . . . see me," she said, "so I . . . hurried back . . . to my bedroom. When I got there . . . I knew I had to . . . warn you."

"It did not occur to you to go away and leave me to my fate?" the Earl asked.

Donela blushed.

"I . . . I did think . . . of it, but I knew Papa would tell me it was . . . my duty . . . and anyway . . . how could I let . . . them . . . injure you? It was . . . wicked and . . . a crime!"

"I agree with you," the Earl said, "and I am exceedingly grateful to you, Donela, for saving me."

He spoke with a sincerity that was unmistakable, and Donela said:

"You will be . . . very careful . . . and warn . . . your staff in London to . . . watch over you?"

"I promise I will do that," the Earl said.

Donela rose to her feet.

"Now I must be on my way," she said. "Thank you very much for letting me stay in your beautiful house."

The Earl smiled.

"I do not remember having much choice in the matter, but you realise it is now impossible for you to leave me."

She looked at him in surprise before she asked:

"Why do you say . . . that?"

"Because you must be aware that you are the only person who can identify my assailants, or, rather, who is paying someone to assault me."

"But . . . I did not . . . see him," Donela objected.

"You *heard* him!"

Donela was still.

"You heard the 'gentleman's' voice," the Earl said, "and I cannot believe with your astute memory that if you heard him speak again you would not be able to identify him."

"I . . . I cannot do . . . that," Donela said hastily. "I imagine . . . all your guests have . . . left by now and he . . . will have gone . . . to London."

"That is true," the Earl said, "and, as I also am going to London, I am afraid you must come with me."

"I . . . cannot do . . . that!"

"Why not?"

Now Donela tried to think of a good reason.

The Earl waited and finally she said in a very small voice:

"I . . . I want . . . to stay in the . . . country . . . it is . . . safer!"

"If that is what is worrying you," the Earl said, "just as you are protecting me, I will protect you, and I promise if you come to London with me, no one shall frighten you."

"But . . . I have . . . nowhere to . . . stay in . . . London," Donela said childishly.

The Earl smiled.

"I have one of my aunts, Lady Edith Ford, staying

129

with me in my house in Park Lane. She has fractured her leg and is therefore confined to her room. She will be a very effective chaperone, if that is what is worrying you."

Donela tried to think of another reason why she could not go with him.

As she did not speak, the Earl rose.

"I am driving to London," he said, "and I think you will enjoy travelling behind my new team of chestnuts. We will be leaving in a quarter-of-an-hour."

"M-must I really . . . come with . . . you?" Donela asked.

"I am sorry if the idea is repugnant to you," the Earl replied, "but I have no wish to be attacked, whether it is at night or in the daytime!"

"No . . . of course . . . not," Donela agreed. "It is . . . just that . . . I thought I . . . could tell you . . . what happened . . . then go away."

"If you will stay with me," the Earl said, "let me assure you, I am deeply in your debt and will do everything in my power to try and please you."

He was speaking without the cynical note in his voice, which made her feel embarrassed.

At the same time, she felt a little shy.

Her long eye-lashes fluttered before she said:

"Thank you . . . but I did . . . not mean to be an . . . encumbrance."

"I think Fate has taken a hand in my affairs," the Earl said, "and let me say, if you had vanished into the night as you wished to do, I would have been deeply perturbed."

"You do not ... expect me to ... believe that," Donela said. "After all ... I only came ... here to ... entertain your ... guests."

"Which you did very successfully," the Earl said, "and you not only entertained, but intrigued me!"

Donela thought of how he had tried to kiss her, and blushed again.

The Earl parted his lips as if to say something.

Instead, in a matter-of-fact tone, he remarked:

"I will be leaving in a few minutes. Is there anything you would like before we go?"

"No, thank you," Donela said. "I have just had a delicious breakfast and my luggage, such as it is, is in the hall."

The Earl looked at his watch.

"I think the horses should be round by now."

They walked from the Study.

As they passed down the corridor, Donela thought rather wistfully that it was sad she had not had the chance to see more of the Earl's magnificent house.

There were pictures she would have liked to study and inlaid furniture which she knew would have delighted her mother.

Most of all, she would have liked to see the Library.

'It is too late,' she thought, 'and I suppose I will never again have the opportunity.'

As they reached the hall, an open Chaise drawn by four perfectly matched chestnuts was pulling up outside.

Donela went to the open door to look at them, then exclaimed:

"They are magnificent! It must be difficult to tell one from another!"

"That is what my grooms say," the Earl remarked, "and if we do not beat the record time to London, I shall be disappointed."

They went down the steps.

Only as they reached the bottom did Donela remember her carpet-bag.

"My bag!" she exclaimed, looking back.

Then she saw a footman was carrying it and he placed it at the back of the Chaise.

"Is that all you have with you?" the Earl asked.

Donela laughed at the surprise in his voice.

"It was all I could carry," she answered.

He helped her into the Chaise.

Then he went round to the other side in order to sit in the driving-seat.

There was a groom already perched up at the back.

As they drove off, the Butler and the footmen bowed.

They crossed the ancient bridge over the lake, and moved swiftly down the long drive.

Donela settled herself comfortably.

She knew she was going to enjoy being driven through the English countryside.

She was also aware that the Earl was an expert with the reins, which was what she expected.

They passed through the impressive wrought-iron gates.

As they drove down the village street, men and women coming from their cottages curtsied or saluted as the Earl passed.

"I think your village is very pretty!" Donela said.

"I am proud of it," he answered. "I like to think that everybody who lives here is happy."

"Do you really worry about the people who are dependent upon you?" Donela asked.

"As a matter of fact, I do!" the Earl replied. "And if that surprises you, I consider myself insulted!"

"Forgive me," Donela said, "but from what I have heard, you have so much in your life and so many things to do that I did not expect you to care about the simple, ordinary things that happen in a country village."

"You sound as if you know a great deal about the country," the Earl remarked.

"My mother and I lived in a small village like yours, although not so pretty, in Worcestershire."

"And what happened?" the Earl enquired.

Donela hesitated.

She did not want him to know too much about herself.

Instead, to change the subject, she asked:

"When we arrive in London, how are we going to find the man who wants to prevent you from winning the race on Thursday?"

The Earl was busy for the moment, tooling his horses round a bend in the road.

When he had done so, he said:

"I suspect three of those who were staying with me last night. The only thing I can do is to see them one by one, and for you to tell me which is the villain."

"Suppose," Donela replied, "suppose . . . I make a . . . mistake?"

"I think that is unlikely," the Earl said, "but of course in that case I shall just have to wait until they try again."

She gave a little cry before she said:

"You . . . must be . . . careful! You . . . must!"

"Does it really matter to you?" the Earl asked.

"I should feel . . . responsible if anything . . . happened, simply because if I had . . . stayed longer . . . perhaps the Cockney would have . . . called the gentleman . . . by name."

"That would have been a silly thing to do," the Earl said. "If you had been discovered, they could easily have made certain that you could not repeat what you heard."

"Do you . . . mean," Donela asked in a frightened whisper, "that . . . they . . . might have . . . killed me?"

"That, or taken you prisoner," the Earl replied. "No, Donela, you have been very sensible, and that is why we have to be careful of everything we do."

"Yes . . . of . . . course," she agreed.

They drove on until luncheontime.

They had reached a large, impressive Posting Inn at which the Earl was expected.

A Private Parlour had been engaged for him.

When the meal was served, Donela was aware that most of it had been with them in the Chaise.

Also the wine the Earl was drinking.

He insisted on her having a glass of champagne.

It was either that or because it was the first time

she had ever had a meal alone with a man which made it all so enjoyable.

Naturally they talked of horses.

Inadvertently, although she was trying to be secretive, Donela revealed that she had only recently returned from Florence.

She found that the Earl had been there twice.

They talked about the pictures in the Uffizi and Pitti Galleries and the history of Florence itself.

When luncheon was at an end the Earl said:

"I have enjoyed being with you, Donela, and I hope now you feel you can trust me."

"Yes . . . of . . . course," she said quickly.

"We will dine together tonight," he said, "and continue our conversation."

*   *   *

The Earl reached his house in Park Lane in three hours and twenty minutes.

He assured Donela it was faster than his previous record.

"Of course," he said, "we deduct the delightful hour we spent over luncheon."

"I am not sure that is not cheating," she teased him. "When the Prince Regent did the record from London to Brighton, he counted every minute between the two places."

"It took him five hours," the Earl said, "and I am certain I could do it in three!"

"Of course you could," Donela replied, "but that would not be a fair contest considering that the roads

135

are so much better now than they were then."

The Earl laughed.

"I see I shall have to polish up my brain when I argue with you," he said.

Donela thought it was very enjoyable to be able to argue with him.

All the men she had conversed with previously, like her step-father and even her father, had lectured her rather than listen to her point of view.

They walked into the house.

She thought that in its own way it was just as impressive as the Earl's house in the country.

"How is Her Ladyship today?" the Earl asked the Butler as he took his tall hat and gloves.

"Lady Edith passed a fairly good night, M'Lord," the man replied, "but she's resting this afternoon, and she did say she didn't wish to receive any visitors."

Donela was relieved.

She was thinking that a woman might be even more inquisitive than the Earl.

She was frightened of being cross-examined as to who she was and what she was doing.

In a way it was frightening to be in London.

There was no likelihood of anybody recognising her because she had been abroad for a year-and-a-half.

She had stayed for only a short time in her step-father's house in Park Street before she had been sent to Florence.

"I am quite . . . safe," she told herself reassuringly.

At the same time, she could not help feeling nervous.

Once the Earl knew who his enemy was, he would doubtless wish her to leave immediately.

Then she would have to decide where to go.

She had never imagined when she ran away that there would be so many pitfalls.

The Earl seemed very pleasant.

Yet she was quite sure he still thought of her as being like Kitty and Daisy, in which case, he might try to kiss her again.

He seemed so charming and, in a way, reliable.

At the same time, she could not forget that terrifying moment when he had come to her bedroom and sat on her bed.

"As soon as this is over," she told her self reassuringly, "I shall find somewhere to go."

She was shown into a beautiful room.

It overlooked the garden at the back of the house.

A polite maid unpacked her small belongings.

There was nothing cold or disapproving in her demeanour.

"I'll press the gown you're wearing for dinner, Miss," she said, "and I expect now you'd like a rest. It's a long journey, as I well knows, from th' Hall."

"We came very quickly," Donela replied, "but as you say, it is a long way."

She undressed and got into bed.

The maid promised she would bring her a bath an hour before dinner.

Donela thought perhaps this evening the Earl would

arrange for her to see, or rather hear, the first man he suspected.

But when she went downstairs he said:

"I have been in touch with my first suspect. He is a young man who belongs to my Club. I told him I wished to speak to him at ten o'clock tomorrow morning."

"Was he not . . . curious as to why you wished . . . to see him?"

"I told him I wanted to discuss the race in which we are both taking part," the Earl replied.

"If he is not coming until tomorrow," Donela said, "you must be . . . careful . . . tonight. Suppose the man . . . climbs into . . . your room . . . or perhaps . . . is hidden there . . . already?"

"I have thought of that," the Earl said calmly, "and while my Valet is with me, I shall behave as if I intend to sleep in my usual bed. But as soon as he has gone, I will go to another room."

"That is a good idea . . . but suppose . . . the man who . . . speaks Cockney . . . searches for . . . you?"

"There are quite a number of bedrooms in this house," the Earl said, "and I will choose one which is some way from my own, which has an effective lock, and where there are no cupboards in which to hide."

"I shall . . . pray that . . . you will be . . . all right," Donela said.

"I am sure your prayer will be heard," the Earl said as he smiled.

The dinner they had together was even more delicious than the luncheon.

Donela found it difficult to think of anything but the Earl and the fascinating subjects which seemed to crop up one after another.

He had, she found, travelled extensively.

While she was quite knowledgeable about the countries of Europe, she had visited only Florence.

She asked him a great many questions which he seemed to enjoy answering.

As dinner came to an end she said:

"You are very lucky to have been to Greece. I think I would rather visit Greece than any other country in the world!"

"I am sure you will do so one day," he said, "and you will find your own face looking at you from many of the statues not only in the Parthenon, in Athens, but also in Delphi."

"I wish that were . . . true," Donela said in a low voice. "Everything about Greece and the way the Ancient Greeks altered the thinking of the world . . . intrigues me."

The Earl seemed about to make some response.

Instead, abruptly he rose to his feet.

"I think we should move into the Drawing-Room," he said.

"Yes . . . of course," Donela agreed hastily.

She wondered if he was beginning to find her boring.

Then, instead of taking her into the Drawing-Room, he led her to the Study.

It was very different from the one in the country.

It was a large room, looking into the garden, with all the walls lined with books.

As Donela gave a cry of delight, the Earl said:

"I knew this would please you."

"Of course it does!" she said. "And I am sure it would take me a lifetime to read them all, which is what I would like to do!"

She spoke without thinking, and the Earl said:

"And, of course, you are welcome to stay indefinitely if that is what you really wish."

Donela laughed.

"You would be very embarrassed if I accepted such an invitation and grew old and grey before I finished the last book on the shelves."

The Earl laughed too.

She started to move from book to book, giving exclamations of delight at each one.

He thought as she did so that she looked even more like a Greek Goddess than before.

Last night Donela had been rather embarrassed at the plainness of her gauze gown when she had put it on.

It was certainly very different from the elaborate "Picture Frock" she had worn on the stage.

But it clung to her figure, revealing the soft curves of her breasts and her very small waist.

She had seemed to the Earl the personification of femininity when she came into the Drawing-Room before Dinner.

There was only a very small bustle at the back to make the gown correct for the fashion at the moment.

Otherwise she might easily have been mistaken for a statue of Aphrodite.

Time seemed to fly by.

When it was eleven o'clock Donela said rather apologetically:

"I am sure you hoped I would have retired earlier than this, and if you wanted to go to your Club or to a Party, you should have said so."

"As it happens, I have been perfectly content to talk to you," the Earl said, "but as you have to be down early, perhaps you would be wise to get your beauty sleep."

"Thank you for . . . reminding me, and that is . . . indeed . . . necessary," Donela replied.

The Earl's eyes twinkled.

"Now you are asking for compliments."

"What I am really wondering," Donela said seriously, "is whether you will see these men tomorrow and, please, I do not . . . want to . . . meet them."

She spoke nervously, and the Earl replied quietly:

"No, of course not, I thought I would interview them in this room and I will show you a door in the corner which is covered with books but actually opens into another Sitting-Room which I seldom use."

He walked across the room as she spoke and pulled open the door.

"All you have to do," he said, "is just to listen and after a few minutes I will make some excuse to join you. Then you either nod your head or shake it."

"That sounds . . . easy," Donela said, "but I am very . . . very . . . frightened in case I involve a man who has . . . nothing to do . . . with it or else . . . leave you at the . . . mercy of one . . . that has."

"You are too clever to do either of these things,"

the Earl replied, "just trust your brain to tell you what is right or wrong."

"I shall pray that I will not make a mistake," Donela said.

He opened the door for her.

When they reached the hall he handed her a lighted candle.

It was waiting on the table at the bottom of the stairs.

Before she took it from him she dropped a little curtsy, saying:

"Thank you, My Lord, for what has been a very exciting evening."

"As it has for me," the Earl replied.

She looked into his eyes, and the expression in them made her feel shy.

She took the candle from him and started to walk up the stairs.

Only when she reached the top of them did she stop and look back.

She had rather expected the Earl to be watching her.

Instead, the hall was empty except for the night-footman.

For no reason Donela could understand, she was disappointed.

chapter seven

"Now you understand," the Earl said, "that I will make an excuse to come through this door."

He paused before continuing:

"If the man is the one we are looking for, you nod to me: if not, you shake your head."

"I understand," Donela replied, "and I am only hoping that we find him quickly."

"So am I," the Earl said.

Donela had come down early, expecting to have breakfast with the Earl, but he had already gone riding.

She was just finishing her coffee when he came into the room.

She thought that, in his riding clothes, he looked more impressive and more handsome than he did at other times.

"Good-morning, Donela," he said, "I hope you slept well."

Although she had been very tired, she had, in fact, found it difficult to sleep.

She was worrying over whether they would find the man they were seeking and what would happen if they could not.

She, however, managed to smile at him.

He went to the side-board to help himself from one of the silver dishes.

Then, as he sat down at the table, he said:

"Am I allowed to say I think you look very pretty even though I know you are a little afraid?"

Donela blushed.

"Why should . . . you think that?" she asked after a moment.

"I am rather hoping that you are feeling frightened *for* me and not *of* me."

Donela gave a little laugh.

"I was frightened when I first met you because I heard how awe-inspiring you were."

"Is that my reputation?" the Earl said.

"Of course it is," Donela replied, "you must be aware of that."

"I thought that Banks and his Belles just thought of me as a rich client of Evans's and wondered how much they could get out of me."

"Now you are being cynical," Donela said accusingly, "and when I peeped at you from the stage the first night I wondered why there was a cynical twist on your lips."

"So you were peeping at me," the Earl said.

"I was very curious about you and, of course, the party you were giving."

She had been talking lightly, as they had talked last night at Dinner.

Now, when she remembered how the party had behaved and also later the Earl, she thought that she had been indiscreet.

Quickly, to turn the conversation, she said:

"I suppose the horse you are riding in the race is well-guarded."

There was a startled expression on the Earl's face as he answered:

"I should hope so, but you are not suggesting . . ."

"It suddenly occurred to me," Donela said, "that, if they cannot harm you, they might cripple your horse in some way."

The Earl put his hand up to his forehead.

"I never thought of that. Of course all my horses are locked up at night and there is always a groom on night duty."

Donela thought she had alarmed him unnecessarily.

"It is just . . . something I . . . thought of," she said apologetically.

"And very intelligent of you," the Earl remarked.

He paused for a moment to look at her before he asked:

"How, when you are so lovely, is it necessary for you to be clever too?"

"I wish that were true," Donela said. "If I had been clever, I would not have run away without planning where I should go."

"But Fate did that for you," the Earl said, "and

I am very grateful that you came to me."

When breakfast was finished, because it was still early they went to his Study.

Donela looked at more of his books.

There was so much she wanted to ask him about them that she was disappointed when he looked at the clock.

"As I expect my visitor will be early," he said, "you had better go into the room next door."

As he spoke he walked to the concealed door which had books attached to it.

He opened it and Donela passed into the next room.

"If you pull the door almost to," the Earl said, "it is impossible for anyone on the Study side to realise it is there."

"Yes, I can see that," Donela agreed.

She hesitated and then said:

"You will not keep him too long if he is not the man we want."

"No, of course not," the Earl said, "and do not be nervous."

"I am nervous of . . . making a . . . mistake," Donela replied.

"I am sure you will not do that," he answered, "and it will not be as difficult as you anticipate."

As he spoke he went back into the Study and put the door into position.

Donela was not as optimistic as the Earl.

She thought it might be difficult to recognise the voice of the man she had heard speaking in the dark.

She moved away from the door for the moment to

look at a picture which was hanging in the Sitting-Room she was now in.

It was one of the Earl of Huntingford in 1825 and a very fine example of the work of Sir Joshua Reynolds.

She could see the present Earl had a distinct resemblance to his forebear.

They were both very handsome men.

It was then she heard a Butler in the next room announce:

"Mr. Faulkner to see you, M'Lord."

Quickly, Donela went to the door.

"Good-morning, Mr. Faulkner," she heard the Earl say.

"Good-morning, My Lord," Mr. Faulkner answered. "You wanted to see me."

"I wanted to talk to you about the race on Thursday," the Earl replied. "I believe you have entered for it."

"Yes."

"Are you riding one of your own horses?"

"I possess only one horse," Mr. Faulkner answered, "and actually it is the second favourite."

The Earl smiled.

"I suppose I am the first."

"Of course, and I suppose you will win."

The bitterness in Mr. Faulkner's voice was very obvious.

"And what are the odds at the moment?" the Earl enquired.

"You are three to one on, My Lord," Mr. Faulkner replied, "and I am seven to one."

The Earl raised his eyebrows.

"As much as that?"

"As much as that."

The Earl rose from his desk.

"Forgive me for a moment," he said, "but I have a letter for my Secretary that must be delivered immediately."

He picked up an envelope and walked across the room to the door behind which Donela was listening.

He opened it enough to hold out the envelope.

As he did so he looked at Donela and she nodded her head.

It would have been impossible for her not to be certain from the way Mr. Faulkner spoke.

It was exactly the same as he had done when he had been talking to the Cockney man in the dark.

There was something in the manner in which he enunciated his words.

While the bitterness he had expressed just now was exactly the same as the sentiment which had been there when he had said that, unless the Earl was injured, he would be bankrupt.

She took the envelope from the Earl's hand.

He moved back into the Study and sat down again at his desk.

When he had done so he said quietly:

"I can understand, Faulkner, why you wish to make sure that I cannot ride against you on Thursday, but at the same time, I have no wish to be injured."

He saw the startled expression coming from Mr. Faulkner's face.

Then, as his eyes met the Earl's, he went very pale.

"What . . . are you . . . saying?" he stammered.

"It has come to my knowledge," the Earl replied, "that you are employing a man to cripple me in such a manner than I will not be able to ride."

He paused before continuing.

"He failed to reach me the night before last, and I suppose he will try again tonight."

"You must be the Devil himself," Mr. Faulkner muttered, "to know this."

"How old are you?" the Earl asked unexpectedly.

"I am twenty-one."

"Then why are you in such a desperate position?"

"I have debts of nearly five thousand pounds and not the slightest chance of paying even a part of them unless I can bet what money I have left on my winning the race on Thursday."

"I understand your reason," the Earl said, "but I cannot allow you to behave in such an unsporting manner."

"There is little else I can do," Mr. Faulkner said miserably, "except put a bullet through my head!"

There was silence before the Earl said:

"I think that would be a lamentable waste of life, and I noticed in the Point-to-Point that you were an exceptionally fine rider."

"That is not much use if I cannot even afford to keep my horse."

Now the bitterness in his voice was almost agonizing.

"I have a proposition to make to you," the Earl

said. "You might feel it is more agreeable than killing yourself."

Mr. Faulkner looked at him without much hope in his eyes.

He was a good-looking young man, but now his face was ashen.

He had slumped in his chair as if he could no longer hold himself upright.

"What I am going to suggest is," the Earl said, "that you ride in the race as arranged but you do not bet even a penny on yourself or on anyone else."

He paused, then continued quickly:

"I think you will definitely be second, which, as you are well aware, will be quite a feather in your cap in Sporting Circles."

"Which will be no consolation if I—go to a—debtors' prison."

"When the race is over," the Earl said as if Mr. Faulkner had not spoken, "I suggest you go to New-market, where you will be Assistant to the Manager of my Racing Stable, who is due to retire in a year's time."

There was a breathless silence.

Then, as Mr. Faulkner just stared at him, the Earl said:

"I will cover your debts if you promise me you will not be so extravagant in the future."

Something seemed to snap, and Mr. Faulkner's hands went up to cover his eyes.

"I—did not—know," he said in a broken voice, "there was so much—kindness in—the world."

The Earl gave him a minute or so to compose himself, and then he said:

"We all make mistakes, and because you are so good with horses I am quite certain you will learn from them not to make the same mistake again."

Mr. Faulkner took a handkerchief from his pocket and wiped his eyes.

"I do not—know how to—thank you," he began.

"You can thank me by looking after my race-horses and making sure that no-one either injures them or me."

"I—will serve—you faithfully—all my—life."

His voice broke again on the words and the Earl rose to his feet.

"I suggest you go to my Secretary's room—one of the servants will show you the way—and give him a full account of everything you owe."

He paused before he went on:

"You need not be afraid that he will talk, and nor will I. No-one will know of this bond between us, and, when you arrive at Newmarket on Friday, my Manager, whose name is Watson, will be expecting you."

As he was standing Mr. Faulkner rose too.

The Earl put out his hand and he grasped it in both of his.

"I—swear I will—never fail—you," he said. Then as if it were impossible to say any more, he walked towards the Study door and let himself out.

The Earl was smiling as he turned to go to the other door behind which he knew Donela had been listening.

Before he could reach it she had pushed it open.

She ran towards him and without thinking threw herself against him.

"How could . . . you have been . . . so kind . . . so wonderful?" she asked.

Both her hands were flat against his chest.

As she lifted up her face he could see there were tears in her eyes.

He looked at her.

Then his arms went around her and his lips came down on hers.

Just for a second she stiffened.

Because she had been so moved at the way he had behaved, the tears were now running down her cheeks.

She moved closer to him.

He kissed her at first gently, as if he did not wish to frighten her.

As he felt the softness and innocence of her lips, his kiss became more demanding, more possessive.

It was then Donela felt as if the sunshine flowed through her body in a golden stream.

It moved from her lips to her breast and from her breast to her heart.

It was perfect, and exactly as she thought a kiss should be.

She knew, though it seemed incredible, that she loved the Earl.

She loved him, and it was love that made her feel that her body was melting into his and his kiss was part of the Divine.

As if what she was feeling was echoed in the Earl, he drew her closer still.

He knew as he did so that, never with the many

women with whom he had been involved had he felt as he did at this moment.

It was not the violent, fiery passion to which he was accustomed.

It was something that was not only physically rapturous, but also spiritually ecstatic.

He felt as Donela did, that they no longer had their feet on the ground.

They were flying high up to the sky and into the heart of the sun itself.

It was so rapturous that the Earl raised his head, as if he could not believe what he was feeling was real.

He saw the radiance in Donela's face.

It made her even more lovely than she had ever been before.

Then he was kissing her again, kissing her fiercely, passionately, as if he would never let her go.

It was only when they were both breathless that the Earl said in a very strange voice:

"My darling, my precious, how can you make me feel like this?"

"I . . . love . . . you," Donela whispered.

"And I love you," the Earl said, "and I have never said this to anyone—I love you."

They looked at each other.

But as the Earl would have drawn her closer to him again, the door opened.

"Lord Waltingham to see you, M'Lord," the Butler announced.

The Earl moved away from Donela, who was frozen into immobility.

Lord Waltingham walked into the room, looking large and overpowering.

His balding head and grey hair made him seem even older than when she had last seen him.

She felt as if she had stepped down from Heaven into a horrifying Hell.

"I am so sorry to call so early, Huntingford," Lord Waltingham was saying as he walked towards the Earl.

He paused for a moment before continuing:

"I am on my way to Windsor, and I wanted to let you know that Her Majesty has approved the suggestion that you should be offered the position of the Master of the Horse. I wished to be the first to congratulate you."

"Thank you," the Earl said, "it is very kind of you."

It was as he released the Earl's hand that Lord Waltingham looked towards Donela.

"Donela!" he exclaimed, "what are you doing here? Your step-father informed me you were staying with a relation who had unexpectedly been taken ill."

It was impossible for Donela to answer.

For the moment her brain would not work, and no sound would come from her lips.

As if the Earl understood something dramatic was happening, he said:

"Miss Colwyn is staying with my aunt, Lady Edith Ford, who is unfortunately not well enough to leave her room."

"I understand," Lord Waltingham said, "but, Donela, now that I have found you, I am sure Lady Edith will allow me to call on you this afternoon on my return from Windsor.''

Still Donela did not speak, and he went on:

''I should be here about four-thirty, and I will look forward to telling you what I was prevented from saying the other day.''

It was still impossible for Donela to speak.

Lord Waltingham put out his hand, and as if she were a puppet rather than a human being, she moved her hand towards him.

''I hope you will not disappoint me again,'' he said.

As he spoke he raised her hand to his lips.

As he did so, the revulsion that she had felt before when she thought of him swept through her like forked lightning.

She drew in her breath.

It was with the greatest difficulty she prevented herself from screaming.

Lord Waltingham released her hand and walked towards the door.

The Earl opened it for him.

''Do not bother to see me out, Huntingford,'' he said, ''and once again my congratulations.''

The Earl saw that his Butler was waiting outside.

As they moved down the passage he shut the door and turned towards Donela.

As he did so she gave a cry and ran towards him.

''Hide me . . . hide me,'' she said frantically. ''I cannot . . . see him . . . and I must . . . run away again . . . please . . . help . . . me.''

She looked up at him pleadingly, her eyes dark with fear.

"I do not understand," the Earl said. "What does Waltingham want to see you about?"

"He . . . intends to . . . propose to me and . . . our marriage has . . . already been . . . arranged by . . . my step-father."

The Earl stared at her in astonishment.

Such an idea had never crossed his mind.

"But Waltingham is far too old for you!"

"He is . . . too old and I . . . hate him," Donela cried, "in fact, I find . . . everything about him . . . repulsive . . . but my step-father . . . admires him . . . so much he will . . . force me to . . . marry him."

She looked around frantically, as if seeking a way to escape.

"I must leave . . . I must . . . leave at . . . once. Oh . . . please . . . please tell me . . . where I can . . . go."

The Earl drew her closer to him.

"You are going nowhere," he said, "and there is no reason for you to hide. When Waltingham comes back this afternoon, I will deal with him."

"But you . . . do not . . . understand," Donela said, "my step-father . . . and my mother, because she always does what he says, have given . . . their permission . . . to the marriage. They are my . . . Guardians and there . . . is nothing . . . nothing I can . . . do about it . . . except . . . run away."

"What you can do is quite simple," the Earl said. "When Waltingham returns this afternoon, I will tell him that you are already engaged to me."

Donela's eyes filled her whole face.

"Are you . . . asking me to . . . marry you?" she whispered.

"I am not asking you," the Earl replied, "I am telling you that we are going to be married because we love each other."

"But you . . . you . . . know nothing . . . about me."

"I know that I love you," the Earl said, "and when I came to your room and tried to kiss you and you sent me away, I knew I would never rest until you were mine."

Donela hid her face against him.

"But then you were . . . not thinking of . . . marriage," she murmured.

"That is true," the Earl agreed, "but I wanted you as I have never wanted anyone before, and I know now that if you will not marry me, I shall be far more crippled than by anything Faulkner and his accomplice could ever do to me."

"I can . . . imagine nothing . . . more perfect . . . more wonderful," Donela said, "than being . . . married to you, but . . . suppose when you . . . know . . . me better . . . you find me . . . a bore or you are . . . sorry you have . . . not married . . . someone . . . else."

The Earl's arms tightened.

"I have never asked anyone to marry me before," he said, "and I can think of nothing more humiliating than if you said 'no.' "

"I love . . . you," Donela whispered. "I love you with all my heart and all . . . my soul. Perhaps after . . . all that has . . . happened I will . . . be able to . . . look after you so that . . . you are . . . never in the . . . same sort of . . . danger . . . again."

The Earl laughed very tenderly.

"I thought I was going to look after you, my lovely. That is certainly something I must do so that you do not get involved with men like Basil Banks or go to Stag Parties like those given by the raffish Earl of Huntingford."

He looked so happy as he spoke that Donela smiled back at him and said:

"You do not . . . think the . . . Earl of Huntingford will be giving those . . . sort of Parties . . . in the future and . . . refuse to . . . invite his . . . wife."

"There will be no Parties," the Earl said, "except very respectable ones in which, my darling, you will shine like a glowing light, or rather like the Star your father said he looked for in the sky."

His voice deepened as he went on:

"You are my Star sent by God to save me, to guide and inspire me. Quite frankly, I cannot live without you."

He did not wait for her reply but kissed her again.

He kissed her until the sun was enveloping them with a golden haze which once again carried them up to the sky.

Donela felt as if her heart were singing with the angels, and she knew that God had not failed her.

She had prayed that she might find love, the real love that her mother had for her father.

God had given it to her.

It was a love that would deepen through the years and go on for Eternity, the love which comes from God and is God and there is no running away from it.

ABOUT THE AUTHOR

Barbara Cartland, the world's most famous romantic novelist, who is also an historian, playwright, lecturer, political speaker and television personality, has now written over 500 books and sold over 500 million copies all over the world.

She has also had many historical works published and has written four autobiographies as well as the biographies of her mother and that of her brother, Ronald Cartland, who was the first Member of Parliment to be killed in the last war. This book has a preface by Sir Winston Churchill and has just been republished with an introduction by Sir Arthur Bryant.

Love at the Helm, a novel written with the help and inspiration of the late Earl Mountbatten of Burma, Great Uncle of His Royal Highness The Prince of Wales, is being sold for the Mountbatten Memorial Trust.

She has broken the world record for the last fourteen years by writing an average of twenty-three books a year. In the *Guinness Book of Records* she is listed as the world's top-selling author.

Miss Cartland in 1978 sang an Album of Love Songs with the Royal Philharmonic Orchestra.

In private life Barbara Cartland, who is a Dame of the Order of St. John of Jerusalem, Chairman of the

St. John Council in Hertfordshire and Deputy President of the St. John Ambulance Brigade, has fought for better conditions and salaries for Midwives and Nurses.

She championed the cause for the Elderly in 1956 invoking a Government Enquiry into the "Housing Conditions of Old People."

In 1962 she had the Law of England changed so that Local Authorities had to provide camps for their own Gypsies. This has meant that since then thousands and thousands of Gypsy children have been able to go to School, which they had never been able to do in the past, as their caravans were moved every twenty-four hours by the Police.

There are now fourteen camps in Hertfordshire and Barbara Cartland has her own Romany Gypsy Camp called Barbaraville by the Gypsies.

Her designs "Decorating with Love" are being sold all over the U.S.A. and the National Home Fashions League made her, in 1981, "Woman of Achievement."

She is unique in that she was one and two in the Dalton list of Best Sellers, and one week had four books in the top twenty.

Barbara Cartland's book *Getting Older, Growing Younger* has been published in Great Britain and the U.S.A. and her fifth cookery book, *The Romance of Food*, is now being used by the House of Commons.

In 1984 she received at Kennedy Airport America's Bishop Wright Air Industry Award for her contribution to the development of aviation. In 1931 she and two R.A.F. Officers thought of, and carried, the first aeroplane-towed glider airmail.

During the War she was Chief Lady Welfare Officer in Bedfordshire looking after 20,000 Service men and women. She thought of having a pool of Wedding Dresses at the War Office so a Service Bride could hire a gown for the day.

She bought 1,000 gowns without coupons for the A.T.S., the W.A.A.F.'s and the W.R.E.N.S. In 1945 Barbara Cartland received the Certificate of Merit from Eastern Command.

In 1964 Barbara Cartland founded the National Association for Health of which she is the President, as a front for all the Health Stores and for any product made as alternative medicine.

This is now a £300,000 turnover a year, with one third going in export.

In January 1988 she received *La Médaille de Vermeil de la Ville de Paris*. This is the highest award to be given in France by the City of Paris. She has sold 25 million books in France.

In March 1988 Barbara Cartland was asked by the Indian Government to open their Health Resort outside Delhi. This is almost the largest Health Resort in the world.

Barbara Cartland was received with great enthusiasm by her fans, who fêted her at a reception in the City, and she received the gift of an embossed plate from the Government.